Timothy's Home

Elaine Littau

DEDICATION

For Terry, Stephen, Marlin, Mikey, Aimee, April, Cari, Devon, Zach, Sierra, Maci, and Raegan. You are my precious family. I also appreciate the encouragement from my brothers- Jim & Maynard and my sister-Geraldine along with dear friends who have helped me keep writing. Thank you.

FAMILY TREES FOR THE NAN'S
HERITAGE SERIES

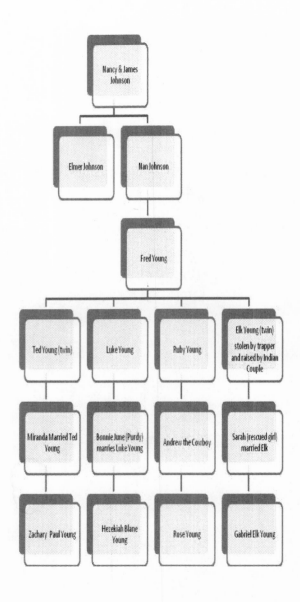

Timothy's Home Family Tree for Timothy Forrester

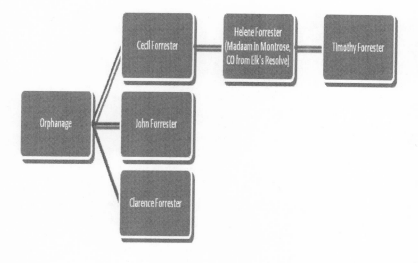

FOREWORD

Timothy's Home, book five, is the final installment in *Nan's Heritage Series*, but no need to worry because another series is in the works and you will get to revisit some familiar faces. It has been evident with each book, Elaine's writing only gets better and her fan base gets larger with growing anticipation for the next book.

Her new main character is Timothy; he is a teen who has been at the mercy of father's abuse for far too long until his uncle decides to step in and save the young boy. The trunk from *Nan's Journey* resurfaces in this story and creates new connections to some favorite characters of the past.

The characters you meet in Elaine's book are no accident. What I mean by this is that each person in her book serves a purpose. Some of her characters are dealt a horrible hand but the one constant in every book is either they have God or they find and embrace God. Abuse, depression, forgiveness, and whether or not to follow your heart are just a few examples of what Elaine's characters face. The reason for this is no matter the time period, these kinds of emotions are relevant today, and will be decades from now. By dealing with issues that are timeless the characters become real and in some cases very personal.

Elaine has taken her writing one step further by speaking at schools, women's groups, churches and various other venues about those very issues I mentioned above. This is where you really get to know Elaine through her personal stories, some funny and lighthearted and some deal with matters that are a little more serious. No matter the story, written or verbal, Elaine's heart is in each one.

I'm very proud of my mother in-law. She is such a wonderful example of how it is never too late to follow your dreams.

Aimee Littau-
Daughter- in-law/ friend

PRAISE FOR TIMOTHY'S HOME

Author Elaine Littau proves herself to be a seasoned and skilled storyteller in Timothy's Home, the final installment of the Nan's Heritage series. Touching, often heart-wrenching, this inspiring novel will make you love her characters and leave a smile on your face long after the last page is read.
Cindy Kelley, screenwriter and co-author of The Silent Gift.

Congratulations! Timothy's Home has many twists and turns, captures imagination and realism, including leading the persons to Christianity.
Andrea Giltner

With each story that Ms. Littau weaves, she grows as a storyteller. This is especially true of "Timothy's Home." I loved Nan's Journey and each of the books that followed in the series. I have to say there is something special about her latest work. There is an element of humanness that touches the soul and leaves one wanting, searching. Perhaps because we find ourselves in the midst of these typewritten pages, our shortcomings revealed, our failures exposed and we come to understand the concept of unconditional love and forgiveness. Quite possibly because we are alone and lonely, without direction and a plan. Whatever your situation, you will find hope between the front and back covers of "Timothy's Home." I look forward with great anticipation to further works by Ms. Littau.

Darlene Shortridge, Author of Until Forever

ACKNOWLEDGMENTS

Writing books is a healing process for me. It brings back times in my life that can never be replaced. It causes me to respect the times I am living in today. Terry and I got married on March 1, 1975. In some ways, that seems like a very long time ago. In others...yesterday. We lived in a mobile home in a trailer park across the alley from my childhood home. Every morning I walked the short distance to Mom and Daddy's house.

Daddy was retired so he was with us every morning and was the one who made pot after pot of coffee for Mama, me, and my sisters- Donna, Geraldine, and Wanda. We laughed and told stories around that happy table. On occasion, our brothers, Maynard and Jim, joined us when they came to town for a visit.

Geraldine was the first to have to leave because she had a job. Soon after, Donna and Wanda left to take care of their homes. I lingered a little longer because Mama let me use her washer and dryer and I had all my housework caught up.

The last day of February in 1976 my sweet sister, Wanda, passed away at the age of 35. That was a defining time in all of our lives. Never had sorrow hit us in such a profound way. Even in the fact that we were Christians, we were so lost. We tried to hold one another up in the knowing that we would see her again, but the words had a hard time sinking in.

Looking back, I see so many mistakes I made at that time. I was 20 years old and had so much to learn about comforting the ones I love. I really dropped the ball with Wanda's children. Even though I prayed so hard for them and loved them from afar, I failed them as an aunt. It is remarkable that they love me today.

Our table emptied one-by-one with the passing of time. Donna and her husband moved and Daddy had a major stroke and died. Our hearts were broken. Exactly 25 years from Wanda's death, we lost Donna. Even though we had been through losing a sister before, the pain of loss was still indescribable. Her children were grown, but their suffering was palatable.

Still, Geraldine and I met with Mama for coffee with her until she became unable to live on her own. She passed away in her sleep at the age of 93.

These days I still meet with Geraldine almost everyday. It is usually in the afternoon and well past coffee time, but our bond is very strong. Our brothers phone us regularly and we are very close. We talk about the days we were all together, but we are grateful for the love we share today. I never want to take my sister and brothers for granted. Even though I didn't grow up with them in my parents' home,(They were grown up when I was born.) my heart is knitted together with them. I love them so much.

If you have read through this I guess the message I want to communicate is that life really is precious. It is important to be mentally present with the people you are with whether it is having coffee, watching a ballgame, shopping together, or just having a conversation. Please, I beg of you, put down the cell phone, stop texting, and stop making mental lists of the things you must do.

These things will always be there...people you love won't. Give them your full attention. Pay attention to how they laugh and talk...memorize these things. Life is like a vapor. (Think of hairspray and how fast it disappears after you quit pushing on the button.) It really does go by this quickly.

Geraldine, Maynard, Jim, and my sweet husband, Terry...you mean the world to me. You are my past and my future. I love you all so much.

Elaine Littau

Other Titles by Elaine Littau:

In the Nan's Heritage Series:
Book I - Nan's Journey
Book II - Elk's Resolve
Book III - Luke's Legacy
Book IV - The Eyes of a Stranger
Book V - Timothy's Home

Coming In 2012
A New Series
Reacued...A Series of Hope
Book I - Some Happy

CHAPTER 1

Timothy held his breath as he peered from behind the haystack. The man he watched tossed his head back with the mostly empty bottle gripped in his hands. The whiskey dripped down the corner of his mouth as the amber liquid loosed his lips and he cursed into the darkness of the broken-down barn. Cecil screamed, "Git your sorry self out here and face me like a man!"

The boy emerged from the safety of the shadows thinking, *I'm too tired to go through this again!* Cecil stormed to him and yanked the kid's emaciated arm almost from its socket.

"Pa...please...!" the boy croaked.

Cecil swaggered across the room, dragging the boy by the galluses of his overalls to a chain hanging from the main beam of the building. He looped a large hook through the overalls and pulled at the chain until the boy was suspended a few inches above the floor.

"C'mon kid...see iffen you can run now!" He grabbed a bridle from a nail on the wall and hit the boy across the face with the braided leather strap. "I said 'run'!"

He flailed in the air with his legs and arms trying to appease his father as leather slapped across his back. *I must watch to save some energy for later in case this one lasts through the night.* "God, let him pass out soon," he prayed softly.

"Cecil! What in tarnation are you doin' to that kid?" John Forrester asked as he opened the barn door.

Cecil Forrester rubbed his bleary eyes and tried to focus on his younger brother. "Tain't none of yer business, John! Watch this...kid, flap your arms and fly away!" he commanded.

The boy moved his arms slowly.

"You never thought you would see a pig fly, did you?" Cecil fell over in drunken laughter.

"Let me take him home with me. The kid is tired. C'mon Cecil...you need to sleep," John pleaded.

"You go home and leave us be! He is my kid and I'll do with him as I please."

John looked at the ground and stepped into the clear night air.

The boy's heart sank. He dared not look into his father's eyes but could not keep from it. A voice, strained and evil, came from his father's lips. "I tried to kill you before you were born! I will finish the job one day."

He looked at his father as if he were a child. "Pa, you don't mean that! I know you don't mean that. It is just the whiskey talkin'."

Cecil's mouth flew open in astonishment that the boy spoke kindly to him. He jerked the chain from the hook and the boy fell in a heap. Cecil left the barn without seeing the damage that was done to the youngster.

*****

He couldn't get the face of his nephew out of his mind. He would have liked to have brought him home, but Cecil was right. The boy was his son and he had no right to interfere. He walked past the train station and wished there was a way to get a ticket for the boy and send him far away. Of course that was impossible since everyone in town knew Cecil and his boy. He dug his hands down further into his pockets. "You're a coward to leave him at the mercy of Cecil," he growled. He could not recall one time that he had stood up to his older brother.

The sound of dogs fighting on the baggage platform drew his attention to the train station. John noticed a large trunk pushed against the wall. The big old thing had been there for years. He wondered why no one had claimed it.

Boston was a bustling city and the station was the hub of all activity, yet this trunk was sitting like an old maid wallflower waiting to be asked to dance. He shook his head and went down two buildings to the blacksmith's shop.

There was no one to greet him as he came through the door. He went through the mundane routine of every evening of his life. After stoking the fire in his wood stove in the small area allocated as the living quarters, he pulled out a few potatoes from a gunny sack sitting in the corner of the tiny room. He scrubbed them with water from the bucket sitting on a table beside the only window in the place. He poured more water from the bucket into an old cast iron kettle and placed it on the stove top. Suspending each potato over the kettle in the palm of his hand, he quartered it with a large butcher knife. He hated peeling potatoes so he decided that he would make his tater soup with skins and all.

A large onion sat in the window sill. He plucked it off and peeled the outer layer and cut the root off. He quartered it and threw it into the now-boiling water with the potatoes. White foam floated on the top of the rolling water and the potatoes bounced into one another. The concoction smelled good to the ravenous man. He liked black pepper so he did not spare when he used the pepper mill. He added a hunk of butter to the soup and poured salt into the hollow of his hand.

The potatoes were softening up and he took a large spoon and broke them up in the boiling water.

He added a splash of cream and watched the butter take hold of it. Ready or not, he was starving.

Placing the boiling kettle on the table, he turned and found his large wooden bowl and long-used spoon. There was bread left over from his noon meal. He was glad he had wrapped it in the ragged dish towel. It seemed soft enough. He dearly hated the chore of bread-making but it would have to be done tomorrow if he were to have any. He filled an old canning jar with milk and the simple meal was done.

He folded his hands and thanked the Good Lord for his food. As he savored the flavor and satisfaction of his supper, his mind turned to his skinny little nephew. Little Timothy didn't have much of a chance. His ma left him on the day he turned two. She ran off with a man who promised adventure. Cecil tended to blame the little tyke instead of the careless woman.

"Dad blame it!" he yelped as the hot substance burned his tongue. He took a big swallow of milk to put out the fire. He finished the first bowl and filled a second. "How can I get Timothy out of town without Cecil knowing?" He fussed around the kitchen cleaning up the supper dishes. "The only way that kid will get away from his old man will be in a coffin."

He sat at the table and laid his head on his folded arms. He pictured Timothy in a small casket and his stomach turned sour. "I can't let that happen!" he exclaimed as he slammed his fist on the table. He extinguished the flame of the lamp as he crawled into the small bed in the corner of the room. "God, help me help the kid!"

CHAPTER 2

Timothy moaned softly as he pulled the chains from his shoulders and torso. New bruises throbbed on his backside and legs, but he got through this episode in relatively good shape. He pushed away a bit of hay that hid the loose board that housed the piece of bread the storekeeper had given him for supper. It had a tough crust, but the starving boy ate it with gratitude. He went to the horse trough and knelt down beside it, dipping his hand in it and bringing up a bit to wash down the stale bread. He stripped off his clothes, eased his tired body into the cold water and soaked in it, letting it cleanse his wounds and take some of the pain from the bruises.

He shivered as he pulled on the same dirty, ill-fitting trousers and shirt. He had outgrown his shoes months ago. There were no replacements. He heaped the straw into a large mound and burrowed into it.

Blessed sleep! Thank you, God. He fell asleep instantly in spite of the cold and the rumbling of his stomach.

*****

John bounded out of the insufferable bed and jerked on his coat as he fought his way through the thick fog. He had to clear his head. Something had to be done about Timothy. A loud whistle arrested his attention and he jumped free of the train tracks and onto the high platform just as the midnight train screeched into the station. Backing away from the boxcar doors as men opened them to stack the freight onto the platform; he bumped against the weathered old trunk he had noticed earlier. It almost put him off balance. The worn tag attached to the handle was barely legible. He blinked against the darkness and read the faded date stamped on the tag. *That's nearly twenty-eight years ago! Where did this old thing come from?* He strained his eyes in reading the return address, Campo, Colorado. "This old thing is almost the size of a coffin!" he muttered. He remembered the words he spoke in the darkness of his kitchen. *It might save the little guy from needing a real coffin.* He raced to the livery and hitched his horse to the buckboard. Returning to the platform, he loaded the trunk into the back of the wagon. *If nobody has picked up that thing in twenty-eight years, they aren't going to miss it now.*

After loading it up, he entered the station to find the ticket agent. The little man looked over his wire-framed spectacles and set aside a stack of papers as John approached the counter. "Is there anything I can do for you?"

"...Yes, how much to send a large trunk to...ah...Colorado?"

"Depends on which city in Colorado you are sending it to."

"How far will ten dollars take it?" John asked.

The clerk frowned and ran his finger down the rate ledger. "'Peers that Trinidad, Colorado is as far as ten dollars will take it."

"Would that be in...a...northern..."

"Southern Colorado, sir."

"Of course, I was thinking southern Colorado. That is where my grandmother lives, southern Colorado. Of course she will have to get someone to pick it up for her since she does not live in Trinidad. She does live in the neighboring countryside, however," John said.

"That will be ten dollars, sir."

John found the lone coin in his pocket and placed it on the counter. "Thank you."

"Here is the tag. Just put it on the handle of your trunk."

John made a hasty retreat to his waiting buckboard. He was nervous. Lying was not his strong suit.

*****

The first streaks of sunlight filtered through the gaps in the livery. John already had the forge fired up and had finished several orders. He was busy with a project when the first farmer came in to check on the status of the harness he had left for repair. "I took care of your harness at first light, Jeb."

Jeb fingered the repairs, asking, "How much do I owe you?"

"Two bits will do."

"What are you working on there?" the nosey man wanted to know.

John grimaced as he said, "Another repair."

"Well then, be seeing you around," Jeb said.

"Goodbye, Jeb."

John held the lock in his hand and closed his eyes tight. "God, is this idea from You?"

He opened his eyes slowly and tripped the lock. It worked fine. The adjustment had taken some time to figure out and more time to fashion, but it would work. "Just attach it and it will be done."

He endeavored to stay within the bounds of his routine so as not to draw attention to his movements. It wouldn't do for him to appear to be "up to something". John breathed a prayer as he watched the street. Finally, Timothy crept down the street and approached the livery. He stood inside the door and cracked it open. "Timothy, step inside for a moment, please."

Timothy obeyed quickly. "What is it, Uncle John?"

"I have found a way for you to escape."

The boy's eyes grew large as he registered what his uncle said. "...Escape? How?"

"Then I am right, you want to get away?"

"I don't mean to be bad, but Pa told me he would be killing me someday. I believe him."

"Timothy, if I get you out of here you can never come back. Do you understand?"

He nodded gravely. "How do I get out of here?"

John took the boy to the back room and showed him the large trunk. "You will fit in here. I got some food and water in here. You must do as I say."

He nodded.

"When you finish drinking from each jar, save the lid. You will relieve yourself into the jar and put the lid on tight. I am sending the trunk to a place out west called Trinidad, Colorado. When you get there, you can open the trunk from inside. See, trip the lock like this."

"How did you come up with this idea?"

John put his arms around the kid. "We don't have much time. Just listen to me. You can find work. Storekeepers and the like always need someone. You might want to go further west. I will see to it that your pa will never find you."

"Oh, Uncle!"

"Get in, Timothy; I'm taking you to the station now."

Timothy climbed in and noticed that Uncle John had given him his only pillow. "Uncle!"

"Git in there. It will be all right!"

He lay down and bent his knees to fit. John put a wool horse blanket over him. "You don't want anyone to be able to say they saw you, so resist the urge to get out of the trunk in the boxcar until you know for sure that no one else is in there. There are men who ride in the boxcars sometimes and they might tell on you. I left you some good air holes so you should be fine. One day I will find you."

The plank door burst open and Cecil bellowed into the darkness of the livery. "John, you got any grub? I think my belly is hittin' my backbone."

John quickly shut the lid on the trunk and yelled back. "You want some coffee and eggs?"

"That'll do," Cecil answered as he dropped his large frame into the only chair at the table. He eyed the trunk in the middle of the room. "What you got there?"

John slid two fried eggs into a tin plate and said. "That old thing has been a sore contention for me. An old lady needed the lock fixed and told me to take it to the train station when I finished with it. Do you think you could help me load it up? It is full of books for a school out west."

"Books! What a waste of time," Cecil grunted.

"Hurry and finish them eggs, Cecil, this thing is supposed to be on the next train."

Cecil sloshed down his second cup of coffee and wiped his mouth with the back of his sleeve. "I'll help you even if you are a mite bossy today. I'll take hold of this handle."

John hurriedly grabbed the handle next to him and lifted at the same time as his brother. "Much obliged."

They loaded the trunk onto the buckboard with a thud and plodded down the street to the train station. Timothy felt certain that his pa would hear his heart hammering. He stuck the corner of the blanket into his mouth to keep from crying out. Bile filled his throat when he heard his pa speak to Uncle John as they put the trunk into a boxcar and walked away. Did he dare believe that he was going to be free from his torturous father? He swallowed hard and listened for them. He felt the train jerk and heard the whistle. He was free.

CHAPTER 3

He woke to the rhythm of the moving train. His legs cramped and with great effort he turned onto his side. There was little room to maneuver but he had managed. The change of position was a relief. Next to his head was a loaf of bread wrapped in a rag. He grabbed it and gnawed on it hungrily. He must conserve his food. This trip could last for days. He had no idea how far away Colorado was, but it sounded like the other side of the world to him. "God, are you still here? I need you more than ever now," he whispered. His eyes grew heavy and he slept again.

After several hours, the train slowed to a stop. Timothy heard the heavy door to the boxcar open slightly as a couple of men climbed inside. A small dog scampered to the trunk and sniffed. "What have you got there, Rex?"

"Quiet down, Zeke! The train feller will hear you! Keep that old bag of bones quiet. Do ya hear?"

"I hear 'ya," Zeke answered.

The train whistled and the wheels were once again in motion. Rex continued sniffing and yipped quietly. "Let's see here," Zeke said as he approached the large trunk.

Timothy held his breath as he eyed the dog through one of the air holes. Zeke tried the latch but it was locked.

"Too bad you don't have any bullets for that gun else you could have blew the lock off and opened it," the other man said.

"Aw, it's probably nothin'. Rex tends to get excited over anything these days. Do ya got any grub? All I got is an apple."

"That's more than I got. Be quiet and let's get some shut eye."

Timothy listened as the men snored the night away. He didn't dare sleep. He awoke screaming many nights so he couldn't risk going to sleep until they were gone.

His legs were numb but he couldn't change position. *I wonder if my legs will fall off if I don't get some feeling back into them.* His mind raced as he tried to make a plan for living with useless legs. *God, please make these men leave soon. I think I will die without sleep!*

After many hours, the door scraped open and the stowaways jumped to the ground just as the train slowed.

The open door allowed Timothy to hear the sounds of the city where the train stopped.

He peeked through the hole at the end of the trunk and watched the door. Finally, the wheels slipped down the track and the city was left behind. Timothy was alone in the boxcar. He tripped the latch and eased the lid open slowly. The hinges creaked and his muscles froze at the sound. He determined that he was alone and opened the lid and let the top fall open. He sat upright and stretched his arms over his head. His legs were dead. He slapped and punched them with his fists until the violent sensation of needles stabbed his leg. Placing his fist into his mouth, he screamed as the feeling returned to his feet. He moved his knees up to his chest and pounded his calves until the pain subsided. He gripped the sides of the trunk and eased to his feet. His back seized up but he forced it into a stretch. He tumbled to the floor from the swaying of the vehicle and found that lying flat on his back and stretching his toes apart relieved much of the pain. He placed his hands behind his head and enjoyed his freedom. He would return to his prison box when the train slowed for the next stop. His eyes grew heavy and he slept soundly.

*****

The days blended one into another and Timothy realized that he was out of bread and water. He hoped that he was almost to his destination.

His stomach growled loudly and he pulled his knees up closer to his chest.

If I'm going to die, this is better than dying at the hand of my own pa. The thought of his father's hatred brought hot tears to his eyes. He rubbed them away quickly. *Men don't cry. I'm almost fourteen years old! I can't cry.*

He heard the whistle sound again. *I wonder where we are now.* The brakes squealed loudly as the train slowed to a stop. After a prolonged time of aching quiet, the door to the boxcar slid open noisily. Men filed into the space and unloaded the freight. "Harry, you have to help me with this one. I can't get it by myself."

"Shore 'nuff."

Timothy heard the men groan as they placed the trunk on the platform. "That's it. Let's get the boss man to pay us."

"...Sounds fair to me."

Timothy lay in the trunk and waited. He pressed his eye up to the nearest air hole and decided that it would be dark soon. Finally, all was quiet and dark outside. He found the latch and turned it slowly. It creaked as it released the lock. He pushed the lid slowly and looked through the crack to be certain no one was around. He carefully opened the lid and stepped outside the confining space.

His leg was asleep and he wondered if he could make it to the shadows of the building without being detected.

He was out in the open and it wouldn't do to be seen now. He saw a horse and rider coming toward him and backed into the shadows of the station.

"Git along little dogie, it's time to settle down..." The drunken cowboy sang into the night as he passed the place where Timothy hid.

"Thank you, God," he breathed. He edged back to the trunk and took out the saddle blanket and wrapped it around his frail body. The wind kicked up a bit as he made his bed between the train station buildings. Happily, he stretched his full length on the ground next to the wall. He had made it to Colorado!

CHAPTER 4

John swallowed the bitter hot brew. The legs of his sturdy chair scraped the wide-planked boards in the makeshift kitchen. He dumped the empty tin plate into the wash pan and stood staring into the boiling water on the old wood stove. The face of his nephew visited him in his dreams and he wondered if he had actually put him in a coffin while he still lived. He rubbed his rough hands against his thighs and recollected that he had bored many small air holes into the old trunk. Surely it was enough. He heard a loud bang as Cecil screamed into the darkness of the livery stable. "John, have you seen the kid? He ain't been around all week. You got him hid in here?" Cecil picked his way through to the living quarters where John stood.

"I haven't seen him. Are you sure he isn't hiding in your barn?" John asked.

Cecil's eyes narrowed as he surveyed his younger brother. "I've looked everywhere. He ain't there."

"Should we tell the sheriff? He could get his men to looking for him," John ventured.

"I don't much care for the law to be sticking its nose into my business. I reckon the kid will show up when he gets hungry enough." Cecil turned to leave and stopped. He looked over his shoulder at John. "Don't think you can hide him from me forever. I will find him."

"I am not hiding him here! Go ahead and look. He isn't here! Let me help you look for him. Do you have any ideas of where he would have gone? Would he go to the harbor or train station to get work?" John offered.

"Who would hire a skinny kid like him? He couldn't tow a sack of flour, much less cargo."

"I don't know what to say, Cecil," John said.

Cecil stomped to the door and banged it open, leaving it flapping against the wood plank wall. John blew out his breath between his teeth. "That went well," he muttered. He returned to the kitchen and noticed the burlap bag under the table. He pulled it out and opened it carefully. Inside he had placed the contents of the trunk.

He hadn't looked through the stuff when he crammed it into the sack, but he reasoned that it was time. He reached in and pulled out several dresses. They were simple, yet attractively adorned.

There were two pair of women's shoes and some men's clothes. In the folds of a tissue were tiny baby items. John skimmed the small baby gown with his rough hands. The softness of it brought tears to his eyes. He wondered who these things belonged to. He reached further into the sack and decided to empty the rest of the contents onto the table. All that was left was a small crocheted shawl wrapped around a large old Bible. He unwrapped the Bible and stared at the cover. It had been years since he had seen one up close. The parson read to the congregation every Sunday, but to have a Bible in his possession was a luxury he had never contemplated.

Slowly he opened the cover. Inside the first leaf were two curls tied with ribbon. The ribbon on the black curl was pink and the ribbon fastened to the blonde curl was blue. He held the little curls between his rough fingers and was amazed at the softness of the hair. He blinked through gathering tears and saw an inscription on the very first page.

*****

"To our darling Nancy on her wedding day, you are our sweet girl. Remember we will always love you. – Mama and Daddy"

So the Bible belonged to a girl named Nancy who had a baby girl and a baby boy.

He carefully paged through the book to find more clues, but found only a note or two with a verse scribbled on it. He opened the back cover and saw more writing on the first brittle white page. The handwriting was small and beautiful.

"Oh God, how can I live without my darling! I miss him so much. Why did he have to die? Why am I left here with my two babies? Am I to raise them alone? Sam has offered to marry me. I don't know what to do. I cannot let them starve. Is it wrong to marry someone I do not love? Will You hear me, God? What shall I do?"

A knot tightened in his throat as the drama of this woman's life unfolded before his eyes. At the bottom of the page was another note, scribbled in haste. It was the same handwriting, only messy and hurried.

"God, forgive me for my poor decision. I am afraid for the children. I fear Sam hates them as much as he hates me. I need to get away, but I am with child. Something is wrong. I feel rather poorly. I am afraid I will not make it through this birth. Watch out for my little Nan and Elmer. I am counting on You, God."

He scanned all the pages to see if there was more writing or prayers. The woman was clearly in despair. He placed all the clothes into the burlap bag and kept the old leather Bible. He placed it under his blanket, away from prying eyes. He had no notion of discussing any of this with his brother. In fact, he couldn't even wear the men's clothing even though they looked to be a good fit because of the questions Cecil would raise about them. He couldn't leave them around in case Cecil searched for Timothy and found them. He stepped onto the busy street and walked to the orphanage. He figured they could always use some more clothes. He didn't want to draw attention to himself so he dropped the sack just inside the gate and walked on.

He wondered if Timothy had made it to the end of the line yet. "God, would you help the little fellow get there in one piece?"

CHAPTER 5

Birds chirped loudly in the crisp morning air, causing Timothy to wake with a start. He looked around him and found his bearing. Standing, he stretched and yawned with his arms flexed up to the sky. His feet were cold and his stomach was hollow but he felt extreme joy in these surroundings.

Peeking between the buildings, he saw a beautiful dark-haired woman with a smiling man stop and look at his trunk. She made a big fuss over it. "I know that is my mother's trunk. See...here are our family pictures!" The man found the jars of amber liquid and opened one of them and sniffed. "I'll be!" As he took all the jars and put them on the platform, a large man holding a tiny baby stopped and spoke with them. The man had a badge on his coat. Timothy swallowed hard.

He hoped he wouldn't be found and sent back home. Pa would kill him for sure. His heart pounded with fear. He turned and ran with all his might to the edge of town.

No one seemed to notice him as he ran from the station. He found a creek behind a large white house at the edge of town. Kneeling down, he drank deeply from the crystal clear water. It was sweet and refreshing. He lay on the creek bank and contemplated his future. He couldn't go much longer without food. His weary body ached. He needed to find some kind of work. He gazed into the clear blue sky and enjoyed stretching out in the tall grass.

Sitting up, he peered through the trees and spied a garden behind the house about fifty yards away. Surely there was something left, even though it was well past harvest. He crept up and watched the house intently. It appeared as if no one was home. Digging into the dirt, he found a few tough carrots and some onions. Eventually, he found a few potatoes. He pulled up his shirttail and placed the feast into the make-shift basket, holding the contents for dear life as he ran back to his stream. Carefully, he washed the dirt away and slowly chewed each morsel. "Thank You, God."

He kept watch on the house through the afternoon and evening. A young girl fetched water from the pump and took it inside. Wonderful smells wafted though the breeze as someone fried chicken.

What I wouldn't do for some chicken!

He heard people speaking in the room.

He couldn't make out what the words were but they seemed cheerful. Tears stung his eyes as he thought of the life he had with his father. He never could recall a word not spoken in anger toward him.

He remembered slipping out of sight in his uncle's stable as a big man came in with a young boy. When the man placed his hand on the boy's shoulder, Timothy held his breath, waiting for him to strike the boy, but he only nudged him and messed up his hair. The boy looked the big man in the eye and grinned at him. They spoke as if they were friends. Timothy's heart cried out with longing for a relationship like that with his own father.

He was brought back to the present with the family's laughter. He groaned and wiped the tears from his eyes. *One day I will have a laughing family. I swear it!* He kept vigil on the house until his eyes grew heavy, then he pulled his wool horse blanket around him and slept with his back against the trunk of a big tree. The night had turned very cold but he didn't dare have a fire.

His body was freezing when he awakened to a sunny morning. He moved into the sunlight and rubbed his arms briskly. Suddenly he heard a woman's voice calling. "There is some fresh baked bread on the porch. If you are in need of work, there is a ranch five miles down the road that is always in need of an extra hand."

He watched from the creek bank. It was the same dark-haired woman from the platform. *Did she see me? Does she know I am here?* She went inside and shut the door. He slid quickly to the porch and took the bread, leaving the cloth it was wrapped in behind. Dashing across the yard, he ran down the road until he was sure he couldn't be seen from the house. Sitting on a rock, he tore a hunk off the bread and ate heartily. It was warm and soft with butter spread on the crust. It quieted his ravenous belly and he gave thanks.

*****

The rough-hewn ranch house appeared sooner than Timothy had imagined it would. A middle-aged woman stood on the porch, peering at him from a distance. "Can I help you, boy?"

"I understand you may be hiring help?" he ventured. His throat felt like it was full of sawdust.

She frowned as she answered. "Ted is always hiring help. He is in the barn saddling up. Go on in there and talk to him."

Timothy squared his shoulders as he opened the barn door. The place was well-kept and clean. "Sir, would you be in need of another worker around here?" he asked.

Ted turned and looked at the youngster. That accent was one he was not familiar with. Smiling, he said, "I am always in need of help around here!

I don't recollect ever seeing you before. You aren't from these parts are you?"

"No...sir...I am from back east," he admitted. Tears of fear gathered into the corners of his eyes.

Ted noticed the pale complexion and protruding bones on the kid. "I won't hold that against you. Let's go into the house and get some breakfast before I tell you what I need you to do. I will pay you a fair wage and you get room and board. Does that work for you?"

Timothy blinked quickly, "Yes sir."

"My name is Ted Young. You can call me 'Ted'. My wife, Miranda, is fixin' to go on the range with me this mornin'. You will be meeting her while we eat breakfast."

They stepped into the warm, cozy kitchen and saw Miranda sitting at the table sipping from a coffee cup. She raised her eyebrows at Ted and he winked at her. As she stood, Timothy gasped. She was wearing men's trousers. He had never seen anything like that at home.

The gasp was not unnoticed by Miranda. "Ted and I are going to be riding fence today. Every time I work the ranch with him, I dress like a cowboy. I can't abide fighting skirts all day," she explained.

"He is going to be working for us. Hey kid, I don't know your name."

"Timothy, you can call me 'Tim' if you like."

Ted grinned widely. "...Timothy the apostle. I don't think I will be shortening it to Tim. That is, if you don't mind."

"I don't mind."

Miranda bustled around the kitchen and produced eggs and bacon. She took bread from a plate and sliced off three pieces. "We can have some jelly and bread with our coffee this morning."

Timothy feasted on the savory meal and drank a large cup of milk Miranda offered. He never remembered having such a fine meal. "Thank you, Ma'am."

"Call me 'Mandy' if you want. I have a feeling we are going to be good friends."

After they finished the meal, Ted took Timothy to the barn. "I think we will start you here in the barn. You can clean the stalls and put in fresh hay. Brush down the horses and feed them. Look around the place and note any repairs that need to be made and we will talk over which jobs you can handle and the ones I need to do. Does that sound fair?"

"Is that all? Are you sure you don't need me to do more?"

Ted pushed his hat to the back of his head. "That is enough for the first day. Maybe on Monday you can help Edna heat water for the wash, but for now..."

Timothy nodded.

"Let me show you where you will be bunking. When you finish your daily chores, feel free to roam or just rest in your quarters. It ain't much, but the bed is comfortable.

I think it is important for a working man to get a good night's rest, so I had my mother make a good feather bed for the hired hand's bed frame."

"Your mother made this?" Timothy drank in the small haven attached to the tack room in the barn. His fingers traced the soft bed covered in a large, colorful quilt. He pulled his hand back carefully, afraid that the mirage would disappear. He had never seen such luxury. His eyes fell to a small table with a coal oil lamp on it. A large, substantial maple rocker stood next to it. The room was flooded with light from two windows. Muslin curtains were pulled back to let the light in. There were pegs on the wall for his clothes and a large, round, crocheted rag rug covered the entire floor. A framed needlepoint word sampler hung over the bed. There were words on it and he wished with all his heart that he could read.

"Are you in trouble, Timothy? Is there something I should know about you?"

"No sir. The law is not looking for me. I haven't done anything wrong," Timothy said.

Timothy watched as Ted saddled his horse. Ted nodded and swung his leg over the large paint horse. He led another behind him and stopped in front of the house. "Mandy, you comin' or not?"

The door opened and the trouser-clad Miranda mounted her horse and waved at the boy. "We will be home for supper. See you then."

CHAPTER 6

Gracie smiled warmly at her teacher as she left the small schoolhouse. The wind tugged aggressively at her mass of curly black hair. She was glad that she had taken the time to pull it back with a ribbon on this blustery day. Mr. Starnes was new to her town and made the dull subjects taught at the barren school come to life. He encouraged competition in the classroom with games and prizes. Most of the children enjoyed the friendly activities and Gracie usually excelled in all of them. She smiled at the girl who shared the seat at the wide desk. Maude was a smart girl and they made a good team. "You ready for the spelling bee today?"

"Yep, are you?"

Mr. Starnes ambled through the classroom and stood next to his large wooden desk. "Today, I ask you to think about what it takes to be a good friend."

Maude smiled widely at Mr. Starnes. "All I have to say about that is to be like Gracie."

"Then think about what Gracie does that makes her a good friend." He grinned. "Now, fifth grade, come and sit up front. It is time to recite our times tables."

The school day ended quickly for Maude and Gracie. They collected their lunch pails, buttoned on their heavy coats, and ran out the front door of the newly built school house. "It is getting colder every day! We better run home so our toes won't freeze off before we get there," Gracie called.

"I'll race you!" exclaimed Maude.

The two scampered through the streets to Maude's house in record time. Gracie waved at Maude and continued to her house across the road. She entered the warm kitchen and ran to her mother, who was placing dough into loaf pans for her weekly bread baking. "Hello Gracie, how was school today?"

"It was the best day!" Gracie said happily.

Emily smiled at her little daughter. "You say that every day. Let me get you some milk."

Gracie sat at the large oak table and watched her mother as she finished getting the bread dough ready to rise before placing it in the oven. She enjoyed watching her graceful movements. *Ma can do anything.* A loud tapping sounded at the front door and Gracie jumped from the table to see who was there. It was Mr. Starnes. "Come in, Mr. Starnes. I'll get Mama."

Emily smiled at the new teacher and said, "Come sit in the rocker next to the fireplace. It is very cold today. Is there something that you need?"

Mr. Starnes sat down and held his brown felt hat in his hands. "This is something that involves Gracie. Ted Young brought a boy to my house last week to meet me and to see if I could help him learn how to read, write, and do sums."

"Yes?"

"Mrs. Randall, would you be opposed to letting Gracie help me tutor him until he can read?"

Gracie's eyes widened. She had never spoken to a boy before. How could she help teach one?

Mr. Starnes smiled at her. "You are the smartest student in the school. I am afraid that some of the older girls would take a shine to him and not help him with his studies. I know I can trust you."

Gracie looked at her mother. Emily nodded and Gracie answered quietly. "I will do my best, Mr. Starnes."

Mr. Starnes gripped her hand in a strong handshake. "That a girl! Thank you Gracie...Mrs. Randall."

They watched him replace his hat and sprint down the road toward his quarters at the boarding house.

*****

"Pop, this is Timothy. He has been working for us for a few weeks," Ted said.

Fred stood and indicated two other rockers on the front porch. "Hello, Timothy, pleased to meet you."

"Yes, thank you, Mr. Young," Timothy said as he lowered himself into the rocker.

Fred opened the door and called to his wife, "Nan, do we still have a swallow of lemonade left for Ted and young mister Timothy?"

"That would hit the spot," Ted said.

"Your mama makes the best lemonade," Fred declared.

Nan bustled out onto the porch with four glasses on a small tray. "Here we go. You don't mind if I join you?"

Ted grinned. "Mama, I have someone I would like for you to meet. This is Timothy Forrester. He has been working for Mandy and me for a while."

Timothy realized the sweet, beautiful face belonged to the woman who had called out to him, telling him that she had bread for him and where to go for work. He blushed, hoping that she was not sorry for showing him kindness.

Nan's eyes locked with his. "I very much want to know you, Timothy. We may have a lot in common."

Timothy could only respond with a nod. His throat contracted and he could hardly swallow the tasty refreshment.

"Timothy, bring your glass and join me in the kitchen. My bread is ready to take from the oven.

That will give us a chance to get to know each other," Nan said.

Timothy followed her lamely into the house.

*****

"The...d...aw...g...r...ran..." Timothy grimaced because his voice cracked as he read the simple sentence. It was bad enough to be this old and not know how to read, much less have this problem with his voice. His face reddened under the tanned skin. *At least Gracie is the kind of girl that wouldn't make fun of me.*

"Timothy, you might not need my help much longer. You really do learn fast." Gracie's smile reached her bright blue eyes.

"You are a good teacher," he said.

Mr. Starnes watched them from his desk at the front of the room. He decided that he had made a good decision. Timothy had come along nicely, not only in his education, but also in his appearance. The scrawny boy had grown some taller and filled out. He had built muscles as well as confidence. Schooling had done him a lot of good. His brown hair and eyes had a healthy shine in them now. Ted was right when he told him the boy was near starvation.

With consistent meals and rest, Timothy was able to learn. Every week his mind seemed to work more quickly. With the exception of Gracie, he had never had a student so thirsty for knowledge.

These two were a good match. "All right, Gracie…Timothy, you need to get on home now."

"Thank you, Mr. Starnes, I will take Gracie home," Timothy said.

The two reached Gracie's house quickly on Timothy's horse. He held her forearm as she swung down from behind him on the saddle. "Goodbye, Little Teacher…" He grinned as he touched the brim of his hat in salutation.

"Goodbye …ah…smart student," she fumbled.

She ran into the house to her room and fell onto her bed crying. "Stupid! What a stupid thing to say!" Her eleven-year-old heart was breaking.

Emily ran to the girl and sat next to her on the bed, smoothing the ebony curls with her fingers. "What is it, baby?"

Gracie sobbed. "I never know what to say to Timothy…only when I teach…I don't know!"

"You really do care for this boy, don't you?" Emily felt her heart could break for her daughter. "We will talk with Daddy. He will know what to do."

Gracie sat up quickly. "No! I don't want Daddy to think I am a silly goose. I just…I just never…I don't know…my words get jumbled up when I try to talk to him about other stuff. He doesn't even think of me. I mean as a girl."

Emily wrapped her arms tightly around her young daughter and rubbed her back gently. "In a few years he will see you.

You may not want him then, but he will notice my beautiful Gracie. You will break many hearts some day. Young women like you are rare. You have beauty inside and outside." She held her at arm's-length and looked into the crystal eyes. "Enjoy your childhood and play with Maude. Help Timothy, just as Mr. Starnes has asked you to. You have more years ahead of you to be all grown up than you have to be a child. Please don't rush out of your childhood days. I need you to take your time and learn the lessons of childhood so that you will be better prepared for your adult life. God has good things in store for you. If Timothy is not the one God has in mind for you, then it will be someone else. Live every day of your life. Don't rush through these next few years."

"Mama, I love you!" Gracie exclaimed.

*****

Timothy brushed his horse and measured out some oats. He put a few forks of hay in each stall for the horses. Tomorrow he would muck the stalls. The barn cats eyed him from the loft. He felt happy and content. The door creaked open as Edna came in to milk the cow. "Timothy," she said in greeting.

"Hello, Miss Edna. How are things with you today?" His voice cracked noticeably as he spoke.

Edna smiled. "You're tryin' to get that voice changed one way er another, aren't you?"

"What do I do about it?" he asked.

"Tain't nothin' you can do about it, boy. It just means that one of these days you will be singing bass with the men folk and not soprano with us ladies," she said as she began milking.

"How long will I be like this?"

She looked up. "A few months, I would guess. You might ask Ralph or Ted. They've been through it. Ain't nothin' to get riled up about, boy."

He watched her as she left the barn. Edna was blunt in her ways but he felt comfortable around her. He sometimes pretended that she was his mother. He was happier than he had ever been in his life. Food was plentiful and he didn't have to scrounge for even a bite of it. Ted and Mandy had insisted that he go to school and do his work after the school day was finished. They told him that his value as a hired hand would be higher if he were educated.

He felt that he lived in heaven right here on earth. Mandy loaned him books to read. Many were adventures of far-away places. His imagination bloomed with each one he finished. The weariness in his bones was a thing of the past. He knelt down beside his bed every night and thanked the Good Lord for Ted and Mandy Young. He was able to go two nights in a row without the haunting nightmares. He screamed out in his sleep only on occasion. His other life seemed very far away.

CHAPTER 7

The church was filled with townspeople. Timothy gladly sat on the pew with Ted, Mandy, Ralph, and Edna. Ted's large family sat in the pew ahead of them. He enjoyed watching Ted speak with his grandfather, Nate, and father, Fred. He enjoyed the way Grandma Martha and Ted's mother, Nan, fussed over him. There were girls that had been taken in by the family. They were treated as if they were born into it. As he reflected, he realized that they had done the same with him. He had never experienced love in the way this family practiced it.

His mind turned to Uncle John and he realized that he owed his life to him. A wave of sadness struck him as he thought that it was probable he would never lay eyes on his uncle again and that his father would never show love toward him.

His dreary thoughts were interrupted by a wonderfully deep bass voice. It was Elmer, Nan's brother.

"This is a new song written by E.S. Lorenz. The name of it is 'Tell it to Jesus'." The rich mellow voice boomed through the air.

*****

Are you weary, are you heavy hearted?
Tell it to Jesus, tell it to Jesus.
Are you grieving over joys departed?
Tell it to Jesus alone.
Tell it to Jesus, tell it to Jesus,
He is a Friend that's well known.
You've no other such a friend or brother,
Tell it to Jesus alone.

Do the tears flow down your cheeks unbidden?
Tell it to Jesus, tell it to Jesus.
Have you sins that to men's eyes are hidden?
Tell it to Jesus alone.

Timothy was enthralled by the song. It was as if Elmer knew his heart.

Do you fear the gathering clouds of sorrow?
Tell it to Jesus, tell it to Jesus.
Are you anxious what shall be tomorrow?

Tell it to Jesus alone
Are you troubled at the thought of dying?
Tell it to Jesus, tell it to Jesus.
For Christ's coming kingdom are you sighing?
Tell it to Jesus alone.

Tell it to Jesus, tell it to Jesus,
He is a Friend that's well known.
You've no other such a friend or brother,
Tell it to Jesus alone.

The pastor stood behind the pulpit and opened his Bible. "Let us turn to Proverbs 18:24. 'There is a friend that sticketh closer than a brother.' The song that Elmer sang so well tells us that Jesus is that friend. There are some things that no one understands but God. We don't even understand the feelings in our gut. We ask ourselves 'Why?' many times."

Nan dabbed her eyes with her lace hankie and Fred put a protective arm around her. Timothy recalled that Nan's youngest daughter had run away from home and Elmer had returned from searching for her with the bad news that she was dead. Timothy was moved by the strength of the Young family's faith in God.

The sermon concluded and the congregation stood. The pastor asked, "Have you found that friendship? Jesus is waiting for you to make up your mind.

He has already offered a relationship with you when He died on the cross for your sins. He arose from the dead and lives forever more. He offers life eternal in heaven with Him, but it is your choice. He will not make you be His friend. I ask you to come up front to the altar and let me pray with you. Ask Him to forgive you of your sins and for Him to stick close to you."

Timothy was a boy who prayed but he never thought that he could be a friend of God. Friendship with Jesus was too wonderful for him to understand, but he was ready to take the step. He was one of several that made the decision that morning.

CHAPTER 8

The walk to Cecil's house was short. John stepped up to the door and tapped lightly before he entered. To his dismay, Cecil was seated in the kitchen near the wood stove.

"What do you want?" he asked as he tipped the mostly empty bottle to his lips and swallowed hard.

"Just wondered about Timothy; did he ever show up?"

"Naw, he turned out just like his good-for-nothing ma."

John shook his head, saying, "That boy is nothing like Helene."

"All I know is that I am not going to waste any more time looking for the ungrateful imp," he said, sloshing the rest of the whiskey down.

John narrowed his gaze and observed his brother carefully. Cecil was rail-thin and looked to be wasting away to nothing.

"...You up for a meal at the new place? I heard that they make a really good chicken dinner."

"I don't know," Cecil said.

"I will pay for it."

"Why would you want to do something like that?" Cecil asked warily.

John rubbed his clean-shaven chin and said, "You are my only brother. Besides, I am hungry and don't want to cook."

"If you have that much money, I guess I will go with you."

After the plates arrived at their table, Cecil realized the extent of his hunger. John watched him dive into the fluffy white mashed potatoes. The pile of chicken bones grew next to his plate. They ate in silence. The waitress brought a goodly portion of cherry pie for each of them, along with strong coffee. John watched the woman as she retreated to the kitchen.

The intense look didn't escape Cecil's eyes. "You going to be looking for a wife now?"

"Why would you ask something like that?" John asked as he locked eyes with his older brother.

Cecil wiped his chin with the ample napkin. "You look like you were thinking about it."

John scraped back his chair on the wood floor and stood. "I may never have enough money to take care of a family. I get by all right by myself."

Cecil stood and dropped his napkin on the table. He rubbed his eyes with the palms of his hands and then stretched.

He felt better than he had for days. "John, come by and play some checkers."

"Checkers?" John asked.

"It has been a long winter and I am tired of ...oh well, forget it!"

"Sure, I'll come for checkers," John said.

The two entered the dark house and Cecil lit the lamp next to the old wood stove. He found the game and set it up on the table. The kitchen was littered with bottles. John decided that the dishes were not dirty because Cecil was more interested in drink than food. "Do you miss the boy?" he asked.

"I will tell you the truth. I am glad that he is gone. He would be dead by now if he hadn't left."

"Why?"

"I swore it! I told him I would kill him and I meant it."

John swallowed hard. "You wouldn't have done that! That sounds like something Father would have said."

Cecil's grey eyes turned to steel. "I know. That beast told Clarence the same thing the night he beat him to death. I saw him do it with my own two eyes!"

Air sucked out of John's lungs. "He was a good brother. Father shouldn't have done it. I should have stopped him!"

"You were too little to help Clarence. I tried. It made him so mad he beat me with the same chain he beat Clarence with." Cecil put his elbows on the table and gripped his face in his hands.

"You knew it was bad...the things Father did...why did you beat Timothy?"

Cecil swiped his arm across the old table and flung the checkerboard and pieces across the room. "The devil is in me! It felt good to be the father with all the power." He laughed wickedly. "...The fear in his eyes...pleading for mercy..." He stood and turned over the table. "I could smash your face in and feel good about it."

John stood and leaned in toward Cecil's face. Locking eyes with him, he said, "You will never feel good until you make peace with God," He put a calming hand on Cecil's shoulder. "...and our childhood."

Cecil spun on his heel and grabbed for a bottle next to the wash pan. Opening it, he said, "Nothing helps me make peace with the things Father did to all of us like this does. I ask you, where was God? Where were the nuns? Was there no one who could stop him? Why would a priest kill a kid?"

John crossed his arms and watched his tortured brother. It was as if he were eleven years old again. "No one would have thought the priest could have done the things he did to us. I am sure the nuns who ran the orphanage didn't know. Sister Opal and the others..." The excuses rang hollow in the small room. He had to leave before he sobbed openly. "Try to get some rest, brother."

CHAPTER 9

John opened the door and entered the dark room. He didn't bother to light the lamp or remove his clothes for sleep. He easily found his narrow bed and flopped down on it. He groaned softly. The sound came from the pit of his stomach. The scene before his eyes played in his dreams many times over the years. His brother, Clarence, crying out for mercy from the middle-aged priest...the clang of the chain as it hit against the beam in the old shed...Cecil standing between the big man and his little brother... They were images he would never forget. Cecil and he could never be the same after they buried their little brother.

The night after the burial they ran away from the orphanage and lived in the alleyways of the city. After they grew up, John obsessed over work and Cecil found comfort in whiskey. They were broken boys who grew into broken men.

John considered his life as the process of marking time. He endured childhood, then passed every day in uneventful sameness. That was fine with him. He had passed his forty-ninth birthday with nothing notable on the horizon. *I'm as broken as Cecil. I would never put a woman through the misery I have seen in marriages. I can spend the rest of my days alone. Sometimes alone is better.*

He stretched out on the small cot. His feet dangled off the end. It had never occurred to him to purchase a bed fit for a large-framed man. He never spent money on items for comfort.

"Dad blame it!" he said as he punched his old feather pillow, trying to maneuver the ancient thing into something he could rest his head upon. "I am just like this old place...waiting to fall into a heap at the end." The whisper into the darkness was followed by a soft snore as the exhausted man passed into the world of dreams.

*****

John saw himself stand and walk out the front door of the stable. With each step he took, his feet stepped higher off the ground. He looked down and saw the tops of the old buildings near his home. There was a gentle breeze, but he did not feel cold, even though it was winter.

He looked at his hands and they seemed familiar. He rubbed his face, no whiskers, and smooth.

He was a boy again. He saw a dim light in the distance as he stepped up through cloud cover. Someone took his hand. It was a small hand. Peering through the clouds, he saw a familiar face.

"Clarence! Clarence, I have missed you!"

Clarence wrapped his arms around John and patted him gently on the back. "I want to show you something."

John stepped back and noticed the deep dimples on his brother's cheeks. He nodded and held tightly to the small hand. The light grew brighter as they walked. *This is almost like the break of dawn...only...it is a beautiful place.*

Clarence plopped down on the grassy hill. He rolled onto his stomach and rested his chin on his hands. The ever-present grin spread across his face.

"Where are your shoes?" John asked.

"I like the feel of the grass on my feet," he said, rolling onto his back and pointing to the clouds above their heads. "Look, that cloud looks like a dog."

John felt happy and confused at the same time. "Where are we?"

"This is my home. I wanted you to see it so you would know that I am happy."

"I hated the way you died!" John said, moaning into his hands.

Clarence gazed at him for a moment. "The dying part ended quick-like. Before I knew it, I was here. I felt bad that you and Cecil didn't come with me."

John lay on his stomach and buried his face in his arms, sobbing, "I didn't want you to die. I wanted to help you."

Clarence moved close enough to whisper in his ear. "I have a message for you. I am happy here. You and Cecil are supposed to make a real life for yourselves. God wants you to walk past the day I died. You have a lot to live for."

John turned his head to speak. He was back on the cot in the back room of the stable. He sat up and rubbed his eyes. "Stupid dream," he mumbled. He stretched back down on the cot and attempted to sleep. He couldn't shake the look on Clarence's face or the warm breath on his ear as Clarence whispered to him. Tears stood in his eyes. "I guess I am going to have to learn how to live."

*****

The morning sun invaded the back room of the livery. John's eyes flew open. He stood and stretched. His thoughts picked up where they left off the preceding night. *One more miserable day in this miserable life! How am I supposed to want to live?*

He pumped some water into the wash pan and splashed freezing water onto his face. Turning toward the dingy room, the despair of his soul washed over him. He rubbed his face briskly with the cleanest rag in the pile.

After stoking the fire in the wood stove, he added a few sticks and poured water into the coffee pot. There was some ground coffee left in the drawer of the coffee grinder so he dumped the remnant into the water without measuring. The stuff was bitter anyway.

What would it matter if he measured or not? Half a loaf of bread was wrapped in a towel on the old table so he picked it up and broke it. He had some butter in the ice box. After slathering a large quantity on the hunk of bread, he filled his coffee cup with milk. That would do until the coffee was ready.

The bread was chewy and filling. He was in no mood to cook this morning. His bones ached and his mind was tired. He hadn't felt this tired in years. He drained the rest of the milk from the cup and waited for the coffee to boil.

His eyes fell on the old Bible he had found in the trunk that he sent Timothy away in. He walked to the cot and picked it up. It had been pushed to the middle of the bed sometime during his sleep.

Picking it up, he thumbed through some of the back pages to see if there was more writing from the woman it had belonged to. He saw a red ribbon sticking out and opened it to the marked page. A faint pencil line was drawn under one of the verses.

"Come unto me all ye that labor and are heavy laden and I will give you rest. Take my yoke upon you and learn of me;

for I am meek and lowly in heart; and ye shall find rest unto your souls. For my yoke is easy and my burden is light."

It was in the book of Saint Matthew chapter eleven and verse twenty-eight. "I wish I could believe! Father believed. How could he do the kind of things he did if he believed what this Book says?"

He sat at the table and shut the book. The black leather was faded but the script on the front glowed. "Holy Bible," he whispered.

Words Sister Opal spoke so many years before came to mind. "There was never a man who lived like our precious Jesus. You must remember that others may disappoint you, but He is a friend who sticks closer than a brother. He will be there when you need Him."

John felt tears choking him so he cleared his throat and poured some coffee. He spoke into the empty room. He would never have called it a prayer. "Jesus, if You are there when I need You, then why weren't You with Clarence! He really needed You!"

His thoughts whirled. *Come to me...you are weary...come...I will give you rest.* He sobbed loudly. "All right Jesus, You win! If You are calling my name, I will come. I don't really know how, so You will have to fix it. I have run from my miserable past for the last time. I am tired and I don't know what to do with myself. Show me what to do."

He laid his forehead on the front cover of the book. It felt soft and warm. A strange feeling moved over his entire body and his tense muscles relaxed. He fell into a deep sleep.

*****

"Clarence, be careful. Don't let Father see you over there," Cecil warned his little brother. "We are supposed to be hoeing the beets. He will skin you alive if he sees you."

The little brother grinned and waved at his concerned sibling. He ran further toward the creek. He had seen several large frogs on the bank last time and he wanted to get a closer look. John scampered after him. "What 'cha doin', Clarence? We need to get back to the field."

Clarence pointed at the big fat frogs and gave John the biggest smile he had ever seen. He had lost his top front teeth and looked comical. John rolled on the grass by the creek and laughed hard. "Clarence, you have to be the funniest looking kid I ever did see."

Clarence giggled. A branch snapped. Black birds flew. Father grabbed Clarence. The world turned dark.

CHAPTER 10

Nan indicated a rocking chair next to her on the back porch next to the arbor. "Timothy, please sit and talk with me for a while," she said.

Timothy sat with his elbows on his knees and his hands folded, looking at the board floor of the porch.

"I wanted to talk with you a bit before Fred brings out our lemonade. You and I have a lot in common," she stated.

He looked into her beautiful face and couldn't imagine any way that she could understand what he had been through.

"I see that you don't believe me. Let me tell you my story. Elmer and I lost our father and mother when we were very young. First our father died in a logging accident. Our mother remarried so that we could survive and then she died.

Our step-father was cruel and married an equally cruel woman. Our life was miserable. I endured many severe beatings, but ran away when they began to take their cruelty out on Elmer. He was only five years old when we climbed into a boxcar and found our way to safety."

Timothy gasped. "You rode on a boxcar?"

"Just like you," she said.

"How do you know about that?" he asked.

"The trunk you rode in belonged to my mother. I don't know how you found it but I do remember the day I saw it on the platform. Fred was sure that someone had been in it and traveled in the train car. I told him not to contact the law because I knew that whoever had ridden in that cramped trunk was desperate. I understand that feeling and I didn't want you to get caught."

"How did you know it was me?" Timothy asked.

Nan smiled and said, "You were small enough and I saw you getting water from the creek that afternoon. I watched for you and figured you were half-starved so I hollered from the porch and told you that I had bread for you."

"You saved my life, Nan," he said.

"Now, you need to tell me your story. I want to help you," she said.

Timothy felt a large lump in his throat. "All I ever knew about were beatings. I never knew why my papa beat me. I thought it might have been because he was drunk all the time but even when he was sober he hated me.

My uncle John tried to help me. I know he left food out for me to find most days. He is the one who figured out how I could escape," he said.

"Where are you from?" Nan asked.

Timothy's eyes narrowed as he thought. He sighed. "Boston...please, don't tell Papa!" he said. "He promised that he would kill me the next time he got hold of me."

Nan put her arm around his shoulders. "Sweetheart, I won't tell. I know that a big secret like that will eat you alive. Now that you have told me, you can be free of it. I understand you and will always pray for you."

He laid his head on her tiny shoulder and cried bitter tears. Fred looked through the window before he opened the door with their refreshments and decided to give the boy some time. He waited a good half hour before joining them on the porch.

*****

"Son, you ready to name that horse of yours?" Ted grinned as he walked up to the corral fence. He watched Timothy's face as it registered the look of first love. The object of his affection was a beauty. "Pristine white with large blue eyes and not a mark on her...what are you going to call her?"

"Chowder..." he said.

"What kind of name is that?" Ted laughed.

"She is the color of the best clam chowder there is," he said.

"Is that so? Hmm, she is your horse so you can name her anything you like."

Timothy studied the mare's graceful movements. "I always did want a white horse. Never did I ever think I would own one for real."

"You earned her, Timothy," Ted said. "You have worked very hard and it is high time you had your own horse."

"It will be two years this Saturday."

Ted pushed his hat back and studied Timothy's face. "Have they been good years for you?"

"The best." Timothy tapped his gloved hand on the top rail of the corral fence and headed for the bunkhouse. He turned and spoke. "…Thanks to you and Mandy."

*****

"Is Gracie here?" Timothy asked as Clyde Randall opened the door.

Mr. Randall stepped aside as he beckoned the boy to enter. "Gracie, Timothy is here."

Gracie hurried into the room and rushed to Timothy's side. "Did you bring her?"

"Yep. You want to see her?"

"Sure."

"This way…I named her Chowder," he said.

The white horse stood at the hitching post and held her head up as they approached. "She is beautiful."

He grinned and answered quietly, "She'll do fine."

Gracie studied his face closely and breathed out slowly. She hadn't realized that she had been holding her breath.

"I know that isn't much of a name for the beauty that she is, but it makes me think of where I came from."

"She is a prize, that is for sure," she said.

Timothy watched the young girl as she stroked Chowder's neck. *She is the sister I never had.* The thought made him grin. Gracie looked up and caught the grin and smiled back.

"See you at school," he said.

She ducked her head and nodded, saying, "Thank you for showing her to me."

He swung easily into the saddle and touched the brim of his hat with his forefinger.

*****

Miranda woke early in preparation to join Ted on the range. She dressed quickly and fetched water for coffee and dishes. As she returned to the house, the earthy smell of potatoes struck her nose and made her feel nauseous. She began peeling potatoes to fry along with eggs and bacon for breakfast, but the feeling returned. She crossed the room to take a drink of water from the dipper. The cool water quenched her thirst but she couldn't keep it down.

She ran from the house and wretched into the grass next to the front porch.

Sitting on the porch, she placed her hands on her face. There was no fever. She sat there for a moment to recover and sprang to her feet. Much to her chagrin, she was overcome with dizziness. Strong hands steadied her before she landed on her backside.

"Mandy, are you feeling all right?" Timothy asked.

"I don't know what has gotten into me. I am never sick."

He noted her brown eyes had dark circles under them. "Are you sleeping through the night?"

She shook her head. "I just can't seem to feel comfortable."

"Maybe you have been working too hard. I will go with Ted today."

"You may have to," she reluctantly agreed.

He offered her his hand and opened the door for her to pass through. Ted entered the room and raised his eyebrows. "Breakfast not ready, Mandy?"

"Nope, not this morning. I can't seem to tolerate the smell of food today."

He rushed to her and put his rough hand on her brow. "It doesn't appear that you have a fever."

"No. I just feel queasy."

He caught a lock of her soft blond hair and wrapped it around his finger. "My pretty one should stay home today and get some rest. Timothy and I can check the herd. In fact, we can cook our own breakfast this morning. Is there anything you think you could eat?"

"Nope."

He kissed her on the forehead and led her back to their room. "You will feel better after you rest some."

"You are too good to me, Ted," she said as she sank into the pillows.

He returned to the waiting Timothy. "She will be all right. It must have been something she ate."

Timothy frowned. It seemed to be something more serious to him. He worried that Ted was not more concerned.

Chapter 11

"Lord God, give me the words to say to Cecil," John prayed as he entered his brother's quarters.

The stench was overwhelming as his eyes adjusted to the darkness of the place.

Cecil lifted his head and looked at John with bloodshot eyes. "What'd you ...want?"

"Brother, I am here to help you find your way back to God."

"Aye once waz loss but now I'm fown..." Cecil sang loudly. "See, I am okay."

John lifted him to his feet and locked eyes with him. "You need God!"

In spite of his drunken state, the powerful man shook away from his grip and punched him in the stomach. John bent at the waist and Cecil pushed him down to the ground and straddled him. He punched John's face until he was unconscious. He sat next to him on the floor and cried like a child. "Don't you bother with my soul, little brother. God doesn't care what happens to me." He put John on his bed and went into the barn and lay down in the hay.

*****

The plank door creaked loudly as a large man entered the old barn. "Cecil, are you in here?"

Cecil moaned and sat up. He looked in the direction of the voice. "I am Cecil. Do I know you?" He studied the man. The face was not familiar. Bright green eyes and a large nose dominated the broad face. His hair had once been black but grey strands were conquering the full head of hair. He appeared to be fifty or sixty years old.

"No, I can't say that you have reason to know me," he said.

"State your business," Cecil said as he staggered to his feet.

"I don't really have any business with you, sir. My name is Will Settles."

Cecil's mind whirled. He had no recollection of the name, but the man made him feel uneasy. "What do you want?"

Will smiled. "Cecil, there is a better way to live."

Suddenly Cecil fell to his knees and began to groan and weep. The heaviness of his soul overwhelmed him and he felt desperate before the God of heaven.

Will put his hand on the shaking shoulder. "Cecil, I have been in your shoes. One day I was working in the old cotton factory near Whitesboro, New York. It was a regular day of work for me until a man came to look over the machinery. He was curious as to the workings of the factory.

As he came into the room where I was working, one by one us workers fell to our knees and cried out to God for mercy. The boss man stopped the machinery and told the visitor to help us. The man was Evangelist Charles Finney. He told us there was a remedy for the sickness of our souls. He preached long and hard as he showed us the way to God. That has been a good twenty years ago and it is as true today as it was back then."

Cecil continued groaning as the man told him of the love of God. "I was told in a dream to find a man in Boston named Cecil. I am to pray with you until you know the truth about God. God is real and He wants you to reach out to Him so He can change your life."

Tears ran down the dirty, twisted face. "It is no use! I can't be good. I have tried and I can't change."

"Dear man, if you or I could change ourselves, we would have no need of a Savior. It is because we are helpless to be what the Lord intended that we need Him so much. For you to take it upon yourself to change is like declaring that Jesus' death on the cross was not enough for your salvation, that in your case, you need more than the Supreme Sacrifice. Jesus was enough."

Cecil's stomach cramped and he bit out the words, "Why would God want someone like me?"

"You are a lost soul. You are His child and He loves you. He would not have any of His children perish but that all would come to repentance." Will explained.

"What do I do?"

"Cry out to God. Tell Him everything that comes to your mind. Tell Him if you are mad at Him and why. Talk it all out. Tell Him you are sorry for your sins. Name all of them that you can think of. Name all of your grief and pain. It is a poison to your soul. You must get it all out. Don't hold anything back from Him. He already knows it all, but you need to say it so that you can look at the ugliness of it all and realize what God is doing for you."

"You will stay with me even if it is bad?" Cecil sobbed.

"If that is what you want. I will be here praying for you," Will assured him.

A loud groan escaped Cecil's lips as he cried. "Oh God, I don't know why You care about me. Of all the lost people in this world, I have been the most horrible. I beat my son every day. I starved him. I hurt him so much that he ran away. I hate. I hate so many people. I hate the priest that killed my little brother. I hate Helene for leaving me. I hate myself because the way I think is so bad.

All I want is to drink and forget. I hate John because he is good." He sobbed and moaned. "What is wrong with me? Why would You want me?" He took a deep breath and yelled loudly, "All right, God, if You can clean me up I will live for You. I am tired of being like this. I can't save myself. I couldn't save my little brother from the man who claimed that he knew You better than anyone.

I guess I am mad at You. You let Father kill him. The nuns let him do things to all of us. Where were You? Did You really love me?"

Will prayed intently for the tortured man.

"Okay, God, I give up. Forgive me. That is all I can say," Cecil whispered.

Will put his big arm across Cecil's shoulders. "That is good, Cecil. How do you feel?"

Cecil looked into the green eyes. "I am tired but I can breathe. The heaviness is gone."

"What you need to do next is to get a Bible and read it. You need to talk everything over with God every day. If you find the old feelings coming back, you have to remember that God will take care of it if you let Him. Go to a church that believes what the Bible says. Do you think you can do that?"

"Yes." Cecil nodded.

"I will be around for a few days to help you."

Cecil's eyes clouded over. "I am afraid I need some help right now. I hurt my brother. He is in my bed. I don't know how bad he is."

"Let me take a look at him"

Cecil led the man to John. Will tended to the battered face and ribs. A low moan escaped between the swollen lips. "You were pretty mad at him, weren't you? What did he do to you?"

"He told me he had been praying for me and that I should make things right with God." Cecil spoke in a barely audible voice.

"I suppose I should thank him for taking the brunt of your wrath.

That could be me lying there," Will declared.

"Is he going to be all right?" Cecil asked.

Will observed the young man squirming on the cot. "I think so. He seems to be coming to."

Chapter 12

Miranda breathed in the fragrance of the sage as the horses loped to the upper pastureland. She pulled her brown felt hat down almost to her eyebrows and spurred her horse into a gallop. Ted called out to her. "Manda, what 'cha doin', trying to race?"

She squealed in giggles as he urged Tramp to eat up the ground between them. When he caught her, she pulled her horse to a stop. "Let's have our dinner here under this shade tree before we reach the high ground."

"Sounds good to me," Ted said as he slid from the saddle.

Miranda pulled the saddlebag from her horse while Ted untied the bedroll from his and spread it on the ground. She retrieved several bundles from the saddlebags that revealed fried chicken, cornbread, and apple pie.

"That there is a feast, my beauty!" Ted exclaimed.

"It is a celebration feast," she said.

"What are we celebrating?"

She smiled and blurted out, "The first of a mess of kids."

Ted's blue-green eyes danced.

He grinned so wide that Miranda was sure his face would break. "A baby?" he asked.

"That is how they usually get here. Not full grown, that's for sure."

"So that is why you have been feeling so poorly these past few weeks. That explains a lot. I was sure you had something incurable."

She frowned and said, "Ted, you realize there is no cure for this condition. Once we have a baby we will be parents forever."

He played along. "That is a burden we will share for the rest of our lives." He pulled her to her feet and held her tightly. "Does this mean that you won't be my little cowgirl helper anymore?"

"It is for sure that things will change."

"When we get back home we will have to tell everyone. I am going to be a father!"

"I will be a mother," she said. "I will send a telegram to my brothers and Papa. They will want to know."

*****

Timothy stacked the last quarters of firewood he split during morning chores. He heard Miranda's laughter ring as she and Ted rode into the corral. Ted slid off his horse and quickly stood by Miranda's horse to assist her. Timothy took the reins and prepared to lead them into the barn.

"Timothy, we have some news. There is no reason to worry about Mandy. She is going to have a baby. I am going to be a father!" Ted slapped the boy on the shoulder for emphasis.

"That's good news. I was afraid she might be dying or something." Timothy said.

"Let's go tell Ralph and Edna," Ted said as he grabbed Miranda's hand and they ran to the hired hand's house.

Timothy observed them and smiled. He took the horses into the barn and brushed them down carefully after measuring out their feed and hay. When he finished, he wrapped his arms around the big Paint's neck. Tramp pressed his head against his caretaker in appreciation. Tomorrow would be Sunday and the entire family would know the news. Timothy was sure the Young family would celebrate all afternoon. He would tell Gracie, also. He knew she would be happy for Ted and Miranda.

*****

Timothy excused himself from the family celebration by telling Ted that he would go back to the ranch to do the evening chores before darkness settled in. Chowder turned down the familiar road to Gracie's house. Gracie sat in the tree swing in her front yard and drew patterns in the dirt with her toes. She didn't see him before he called her name. Looking up, she blushed. "Hello, Timothy. You caught me by surprise," she said.

The breeze caught a lock of her curly black hair and blew it away from her porcelain face. Timothy hadn't noticed how clear and sweet her shining blue eyes were before. She was rather pretty with the bright color that stole into her cheeks. "Ted and Miranda are going to have a baby. That is why she has been so sick."

Gracie stood quickly and said, "How sweet...a little baby!"

"Yep, that's what it was," Timothy said, suddenly feeling awkward with the topic in front of the pretty girl. "I need to get back to the ranch."

"Thank you for telling me. I have been concerned for Miranda's health," Gracie said.

He mounted his horse and tipped his hat to her. It struck him that little Gracie had grown up before his eyes and he had never noticed.

His mind was occupied as he sauntered through the end of town. The train whistle caught his attention and he watched it pull away from the station. A few passengers filed down the steps of the platform. He observed them for a moment. Suddenly fear gripped his throat. The stance of one of the passengers was familiar. He would know that walk anywhere. Sweat stood on his brow as he whipped Chowder into a full run. He had to get away. Had Uncle John told Pa where he was? He had to get as far from Trinidad as possible.

Chapter 13

Guilt possessed him as he watered the exhausted horse. He had pushed Chowder for days and hadn't seen that she got decent rest or feed. Tonight, even if his pa caught up to him, the horse would get what she deserved. He pulled the coins from his vest and handed them to the stable boy. "Is that enough to allow me to bed down in here, too?"

"Shore 'nuff. I don't see why not," the kid said.

He took the bedroll and spread it on the floor. Soon he was sound asleep.

Daybreak exploded with the sound of gunfire. Chowder spooked as Timothy leapt to his feet to calm her. Four rough men rode into the stable and hid behind the door.

"Chuck, load up on oats. We need to keep these old nags nourished," the apparent leader ordered.

The man dismounted and took a half-filled gunny sack and tied it on his saddle horn. He glanced around the darkened barn for more supplies when he made eye contact with Timothy. "There's someone in here."

The leader jerked his head in Timothy's direction and aimed his gun at him. "You have two choices, kid. You can join us or …ah…die. I'd say you best saddle that horse and get ready to ride with us."

Timothy obeyed and mounted Chowder.

"Let's go! Now…run!"

They burst out of the barn and ran the horses at break-neck speed until they had put great distance between them and the town. They only stopped for water, traveling until sundown the following day. They were up before sunup and kept moving. Timothy was hungry and tired. His thoughts were scrambled. *How did I get myself into this mess? How am I going to get out of it?*

The leader pulled his horse up to Timothy's and declared, "Don't think you can run out on us. The only way you will ever leave is with a bullet through your heart."

He would have to die to ever get away? He slumped in his saddle. *Get me out of this, God!*

They covered his eyes with a bandana as the horses struggled inch by inch until they stopped on top of a mountain pass. All the riders except Timothy dismounted and led their horses down a steep trail that ended up at a large cave.

Pulling the saddles off their mounts and placing them on a fallen log, the men staggered to a small creek to water their horses.

One of the men uncovered his eyes. THIS MUST BE THEIR HIDE-OUT. Timothy unsaddled Chowder and gave her some oats and led her to the creek. The water was clear and cold. He stooped and drank deeply. His throat was dry and sore. The moisture soothed it. He sat and watched Chowder as she drank and wondered what would happen next.

The outlaw known as Chuck tossed him a slab of jerky. He gnawed on it hungrily.

"The old man ain't all bad. He gives us our cut and keeps us safe. Just don't try to run away," Chuck said.

Timothy chewed the jerky and nodded. He didn't want Chuck to suspect that he might try to run away. He didn't have a plan, but he didn't want to stay with the bunch and be an outlaw.

"The Old Man" strode across the camp with a large bottle of whiskey gripped in his hand. He observed Timothy seated on the ground next to the creek. "You will help our cook. You best get busy."

Timothy stood and walked to the fire pit. "Where is the cook?"

"...Yonder in the cave. She ain't much to look at, but she keeps our bellies full."

Timothy peered into the darkness of the cave.

"Victoria, you got work to do!" the man yelled.

The woman emerged from the refuge and into the open. She held her hand up to shade her eyes. Timothy decided that she was probably old enough to be his mother. She looked as weary as he felt. Long black strings of hair fell from a messy wad of hair at the top of her head.

"I will get the fire going and have supper ready soon," Timothy said.

She frowned. "Kid, don't do me any favors."

"The Old Man" growled at her, saying, "The kid will help you cook. We have no use for him otherwise, unless you want his killin' on yer head."

"Go ahead; let me see what you can do," she said.

He picked up some brush from scrub cedars and some larger branches and began the task of building up a fire for cooking. Chuck tossed him a coffee pot and he filled it with water from the creek. He opened a saddle bag next to the fire and revealed a sack of coffee, beans, flour and other supplies. He reached into the bag of coffee, put a handful into the water, and set it on the fire to boil. Finding a large pot, he filled it with water and put some beans into it to soak. He carved a few slices of bacon from the slab that was wrapped in a flour sack. He placed the slices in a large cast iron skillet at the edge of the fire. He mixed a bit of grease from the bacon and flour together and patted out some flat bread. After the bacon was done, grease popped in the pan and he placed the discs into the skillet. He hoped the meal was good enough. "The beans won't be ready before morning, but you can eat the rest," he said.

The men were hungry and uncomplaining as they finished every morsel that he prepared. Victoria sniffed and nodded her head as she returned to the cave. He decided that he must have passed the test.

*****

The Old Man stood over Timothy and kicked him in the side. "It is high time you go on a raid with us, greenhorn."

Timothy scooted out of the bedroll, trying not to favor his bruised side.

"Get that fancy horse and trail it behind one of the nags. We don't need a calling card when we come to town. You have to sell it."

"Sir?"

The man spit tobacco at Timothy's feet. "You heard me, boy," he said.

Timothy saddled an ancient horse and put a bridle on Chowder. He sat carefully in the saddle and tied the lead rope to his saddle horn.

Chuck put a potato sack over the boy's head, saying, "We don't want you to know the trail."

"Quit jawin' or I'll gun you down where you stand," the leader said.

It was slow going on the trail down the mountain. Timothy felt the sun on his right cheek at times. Most of the time they were in dense forest and no sun hit his face. He tried to determine the direction they traveled, but it seemed that the steep trail wound around a mountain. He found it difficult to remain in the saddle due to the incline. He was not an experienced rider. His heart thumped loudly in his chest. *Don't be afraid. They can smell fear!*

They came to the outskirts of a small settlement. The Old Man told him and Chuck to go to the livery stable and sell Chowder. He and the rest of the 'boys' would wait under the hanging tree.

"Keep your mouth shut, kid. Nobody around here talks like you and we don't need you to seem anything but normal. I will do the barterin'."

The blacksmith looked the creamy white horse over closely. "What 'da want fer her?"

"Ten dollars will set well with me," Chuck said.

"Hmmm...stolen?"

"No, we just need the money...came into some hard times."

The large, dirty man rubbed his hands across his heavy leather apron and crossed his arms. He stretched his neck and tipped back his head, looking down his massive nose at the young boy, saying, "This your horse, kid?"

Timothy opened his mouth and caught Chuck's warning look. He closed his mouth into a hard line and nodded his head.

"It's a deal, then," the blacksmith said.

The two rode up to the group of outlaws and Chuck threw the ten dollar gold piece to the boss.

"Cover his head, Chuck. We have a ways to go before nightfall."

They kept the horses at a walk throughout the daytime hours. It seemed to Timothy that they were on flat land. He smelled the scent of sagebrush. *This must be the area Ted called 'the High Desert'*.

They ate cold beans and cornbread and washed it down with stout coffee. The campfire was small and the men crowded around it with their bedrolls. Chuck led Timothy to a tree and tied his hands behind his back. "If you need to go, just wet yourself."

The Old Man laughed until his sides ached. "Did you ferget the diapers, Chuck?" he asked.

The others joined in the taunting. Timothy wished he could disappear. One by one they tired of making sport of him and settled in for the night. The night rang out with their various snores. He pulled against the rope. It had a bit of slack in it. *Maybe I can get loose...and get away.*

It took a good two hours to free his hands. His arms hurt from being tied at the odd angle. He moved very slowly as he reached for his ankles to undo the rope binding them. Chuck hadn't worked very hard tying that knot. It practically fell away from his legs.

Chuck turned over and groaned loudly. Some of the others shuffled in their bedrolls. The guard was asleep. Timothy heard The Old Man tell him that if he slept on his watch, he would shoot him. *Poor soul...*

He stood and backed out from the circle of the sleeping men. It was pitch dark and there was very little cover across the landscape. He walked carefully for ten paces and crouched behind a soapweed. *No one has missed me yet.* He quickly darted from sagebrush to soapweed, making his way across the desert.

The moon rose overhead and lit up the night. *Oh no! This is as bright as daylight!* He pressed himself close to a cactus and listened. A single gunshot rang through the night. He heard shouting and the sound of hoof beats. He jumped up and ran with every reserve of energy he possessed.

The horses ate up the distance across the wide desert in no time. Chuck threw his lasso around Timothy as if he were a calf ready for the branding iron. Timothy ate a mouthful of dirt when he landed on his face.

"You caused Sully his life. You ain't worth it. Do ya hear me! I would jist as soon shoot you here and now as to look at you. Don't give me any excuses!" he yelled.

Chapter 14

Cecil gripped the valise in his hand and glanced over at his brother. "John, are you sure this was the town you sent the trunk to?"

"The very one..." he answered.

He breathed in the clear air and looked down the length of the street. His mind was clear. He spotted a hotel. "Hey John, let's get a room and pick up the search tomorrow morning."

"I am beat," John said.

The station clerk peered over his spectacles at the men who stood at his window. "Can I help you fellers?"

"Yes, we are looking for a young boy. He is my son," Cecil said.

"From the sound of your speech, I would say that you are not from these parts.

Would your kid be soundin' somewhat like you?" he said as he pushed his spectacles up to his eyes to get a better look.

Cecil nodded. "I suppose he sounds just like me. Do you know him?"

"I be wonderin' what he is doing so far from home," he said.

Cecil looked at John and back at the man and said, "He was running away from me. I want to find him to make things right with him."

"Is that right...hmmm..." The man rubbed his smoothly shaved chin. "He has been working for Ted Young at his ranch. He seems to be a real good boy."

After the station clerk gave the men directions to the Young ranch, they went to the livery stable to get some horses.

"Cecil, maybe I should go alone. Timothy doesn't know that you are a changed man yet. I say that you hang back about an hour and then come to the ranch. I will tell the boy that he can trust you now."

Cecil hung his head and nodded. "It is very wrong for a boy to fear his father. I see the wisdom in what you say. I will be at the ranch an hour after you arrive. John, do you think the boy will hear me out?"

"Timothy loves you. Of course he is afraid of you, but I know that he loves you. He will hear you out."

*****

John knocked on the ranch house door and waited. The door opened with a creak. "Ma'am, I am looking for my nephew, Timothy. I heard that he is working for you at your ranch."

The man with the familiar accent looked kind enough, but Miranda feared for Timothy because she knew the things he had been through. She nodded and opened the door, indicating chairs at the large round table.

"I am the one who put him in the old trunk and sent him to Colorado. I had to get him away from his father. I am sorry, Mrs. Young, my name is John Forrester."

Miranda scurried to the coffee pot and filled a cup for her guest. "I am glad you rescued him. He is a good boy."

"His father, Cecil, is with me," he said as he took the cup.

Miranda dropped into the chair. "You can't mean it! He is with you? Where is he?"

John took a deep breath. "He will be here directly. I have to tell you that he is a changed man. He has seen the error of his ways and wants to make amends."

"It must have been some kind of miracle," she said, fussing with the loose blond hair that wisped around her face.

"May I talk with Timothy?" John asked.

"Ted left out for the far pasture this morning. Timothy didn't come in for breakfast so he probably met him out there. I can take you to his quarters."

"Thank you," John said as he fell into step with her as they headed toward the barn. He stepped into the small room and noted the evidence of the boy. He realized then how much he had missed him. "How is he faring? Has he grown much?"

Miranda laughed. "Goodness sakes, that boy did go through a growing spell. He is taller than me now. Working on the ranch has toughened him up a bit. He has regular muscles and has put on some weight. I guess he likes Edna's cooking."

"Good for him!" he said.

They both turned as they heard Cecil's horse approach. "Cecil, we are over here," John called out.

Cecil turned his horse toward the barn. Miranda couldn't help but fear the powerful man riding up to them. He threw his leg over the back of the horse, landed softly on the ground, and stood before them. "Ma'am, is this where my Timothy lives?"

"Mrs. Young, this is my brother, Cecil Forrester. He is Timothy's father." John made the quick introductions.

"Of course, Mrs. Young, pardon me. I am his father." Cecil seemed flustered.

"Mr. Forrester, I am glad to know you." Miranda offered her hand for a handshake.

"Mr. Young and Timothy are at another area of the ranch right now. This is the room where he lives," John said.

Cecil looked at the room and sat on the bed. He put his head in his hands and sobbed.

Looking up, he said, "Do you think it is too late for me to make things right with him?"

"He has grown up a little. I think he always knew it was the whiskey," John said.

Cecil moaned. "The whiskey didn't do the brutal things to that boy. I did it! I knew I was doing it. I was a hate-filled man. I took out all the hate on my own son. He has every right to hate me. He has every right..." he broke into bitter tears.

"Mr. Forrester, I understand that you are a changed man. If that is true, Timothy will give you another chance."

"I made things right with the Lord. After that, I had to make things right with my son."

Miranda nodded in agreement. "Come into the house and have some coffee. Ted and Timothy should be here for the noon meal. There is plenty. We are having cornbread and beans."

"Thank you, ma'am." John said.

They followed her to the cozy farmhouse and sat at the large oak table. She poured them cups of coffee and presented them with ample slices of cherry pie. "I just baked a couple of these pies this morning. I suppose the Lord knew we were going to have company today," Miranda said.

Cecil poked a small forkful of the delicacy in his mouth. He had never tasted anything like it before. The crust was light and flakey and the fruit was sweetened to perfection. He cast a glance at his brother and laughed aloud. "This is the nectar of the angels. Am I right, John?"

John frowned. "Don't bother me with talking; I want to concentrate on this rare treat. Mrs. Young, we have never had anything as good as this in our lives."

Miranda chuckled. "That is the sweetest compliment I have ever had on my baking."

The two men polished off the whole pie. Miranda didn't withhold one bite from them. They watched her curiously.

"No wonder the boy is growing if he eats like this all the time," John said.

Miranda took their plates and refilled their cups with more coffee. "We usually just eat plain old food. He eats plenty because he is a growing boy."

The sound of hoof beats interrupted their conversation. Miranda opened the door to let Ted and Timothy in. Ted was alone. "Did you run onto Timothy?" she asked.

"Nope, he wasn't in the far pasture. He ..." Ted stopped in mid sentence when he saw Cecil and John standing behind Miranda.

"Ted, this is Timothy's father, Cecil, and his Uncle John."

"Hello."

"Pleased to meet you, Mr. Young," John said, extending his hand for a handshake.

Cecil nodded toward Ted. "Mr. Young."

"I don't know what to make of Timothy's being gone this morning. He is a regular working man. He is my top hand these days.

It isn't like him to not show up where he is needed. I know we talked about working the far pasture last night."

"Can you think of anywhere we need to look? We will help you," Cecil said.

"You can trail along with me today. I don't really know where else to look," Ted answered.

Chapter 15

Tears threatened yet again, but Gracie refused to let them surface. Her eyes drifted to the pew where the Young family sat each Sunday. The spot where Timothy had sat was unoccupied for six months already. She was unable to forget him, but she couldn't get over the way he just up and left. He never told her 'goodbye'. Maybe she had let her childish heart think he cared for her. She was just a schoolmate. She had to forget him. It was obvious that he had forgotten her.

Standing for the closing prayer, she prayed for his safety. She accompanied her mother through the door of the small white church and into the sunlight. The heat of the day was upon them. She shook the pastor's hand, turned, and saw Miranda holding her newborn baby boy.

"Have you heard any word from Timothy?" Miranda asked.

Gracie swallowed hard. "I guess that means that you haven't either. I wonder what happened to him," she said quietly.

"Ted and the family have searched high and low for him without a trace. I told you before that he didn't take one thing with him.

85

It is like he vanished into thin air," Miranda said.

"Are you ready to go?" Gracie's mother asked.

Gracie touched the wee baby lightly on the nose and said, "He is beautiful. I know you are a good mother."

"Thank you, Gracie. We are very happy with little Zachary Paul," she said.

Gracie took her mother's arm and concentrated on the sound of the gravel rocks crunching under her shoes. She cast a sideways glance at her mother and said, "I can't figure out where Timothy went to. Miranda and Ted don't know either."

"You need to think about something else, Gracie. Surely there are other boys you have taken a liking to," she said.

"I don't think about boys. I only wonder what could have happened to Timothy."

Emily Randall studied Gracie's face. "Your father asked Phillip Masters to take Sunday dinner with us. He has asked permission to court you."

Bright color flashed up the side of her neck and into her cheeks. "Mother!" Gracie exclaimed.

"Papa thinks it would be good for you to see him. He never was fond of Timothy. He knows Phillip's family and they are good people."

"...but Mama!"

"Let's get to the house and finish putting out the food. We don't want to keep everyone waiting. You really have no choice in the matter."

Gracie blinked away tears as she set the table, adding an extra plate for Phillip. Her stomach was drawn into a hard knot and she found it hard to swallow. She poured cool milk into each tumbler and placed folded cloth napkins next to each of her mother's best plates. Everyone took his chair as Mr. Randall indicated Phillip's place to him. Emily placed a heaping platter of fried chicken in the center of the table as she sat down. Everyone joined hands as Clyde asked the blessing over the food.

Phillip smiled at Gracie, noticing that her porcelain complexion was enhanced by the high color in her cheeks. Wisps of black ringlets framed her face while the rest of her curly hair was braided into one long heavy braid down her back. Her crystal blue eyes filled with tears as she quickly looked down to her empty plate.

"Gracie, please pass the potatoes and I need some of that butter too," said her father.

Gracie was glad that her mother and father were talkative so that she wouldn't have to say much. Eventually, she stood and gathered empty plates, taking them to the wash pan in the kitchen. She reached for the potholder to hold on the handle of the bucket of boiling water on the wood stove. Her mother scurried into the kitchen and yanked the potholder from her hand. "Gracie, Phillip wants you to go for a walk with him. I will do this."

"...but Mama..."

"I said go!"

Gracie knew she was outnumbered.

She turned as Phillip walked into the kitchen. "Mrs. Randall, I hope you don't mind if I take Gracie for a walk."

Phillip held Gracie firmly on the elbow as they strolled down the dirt road past the houses that flanked her childhood home. Neighbors nodded at the couple from their front porches as the couple walked in silence down the street. Phillip smiled and tipped his hat as they passed each neighbor. Gracie observed him with interest. *He is a friendly fellow. I wish I could think of something interesting to say.*

"Gracie, you don't know me very well. I hope to change that. If you wouldn't mind, I would like to come a courting. You are not only a fetching-looking girl, but also have a sweet soul."

"I, ah, don't know what to say."

"Just say that it would be all right if I get to know you better. Maybe after you know me more, you might find something to like about me," he said with a broad smile across his face.

Chapter 16

Gracie responded to the crisp knock on the front door. Phillip arrived like clockwork for the past six months. She smiled as she opened the door. She noticed that his raven-black hair was carefully combed as he removed the soft brown felt cowboy hat. She decided that he was handsome even though his ever-ready smile was too big for his thin face.

"Can I take your hat?" she asked.

"Thank you, my dear Gracie."

She tilted her head back to see his brown eyes. *He is almost too tall! He is very sure of himself.* She took his hat and placed it on a hook next to the front door. "Please have a seat. I will get you some fresh buttermilk if you like," she said.

"Wonderful."

As he watched her retreat into the kitchen, Mrs. Randall greeted him, "Phillip, how are you faring today?"

"Today is a good day. I have been looking at the homeplace my grandfather left to me. It is a good size farm and the old barn seems to be in good repair."

"That is good."

"Would you tell Mr. Randall that I will be wanting to have a word with him? It is about Gracie's future."

"I will get him," she said as she went in search of her husband.

Gracie brought a tumbler of buttermilk to Phillip and offered him a seat next to the fireplace. "The buttermilk tastes extra good today," she said.

He took a quick sip and smacked his lips. "Too true, this is really good. It hits the spot."

She chuckled when she noticed a small milk mustache on his lips.

"What is it?" he said as he wiped his mouth with the back of his hand.

"Nothing."

Mr. Randall cleared his throat. "I understand you would like a word with me?" he asked.

"Yes."

"Gracie, will you see if your mother needs help in the kitchen?" Mr. Randall asked.

Gracie looked from Phillip to her father and went into the kitchen in search of her mother.

"I have been seeing Gracie and grown very fond of her."

"Yes, she is a lovely girl," Mr. Randall said.

"I am asking you for her hand in marriage."

"Just when were you wanting this marriage to take place?"

Phillip eyed his future father-in-law for a long moment. "Would a year-long engagement be sufficient?" he asked carefully.

Mr. Randall rubbed his chin thoughtfully. "If Gracie is in agreement, I would think a year would be enough time. I suppose I ought to go get her so you can see what her answer is," he said.

Gracie glided into the room and sat in the rocker next to Phillip.

Phillip confidently took her hand and stroked the long fingers. His dancing chocolate-brown eyes met her sky-blue ones. "I would love for you to become my wife. Would you?"

She swallowed through the lump in her throat. "Yes," she whispered.

"I know that a formal engagement should be for at least a year, but I wonder if we could possibly move the wedding up by six months."

"Why?" she asked.

"My grandfather left me his farm, but I want to homestead the land next to it. If we are married, I can get another allotment with it and we can make our farm that much bigger. Our future hinges on this six months! Each plot is one hundred sixty acres. If you filed also, we could have another one hundred sixty. We would have to put improvements on both plots. The cost is twelve and a half cents per acre but we can pay for them in four installments. We have to get a deed of title and build on them." he said.

She looked at his eyes. There was a hint of desperation in them...and...something else. *What is it?*

He focused his eyes on his feet and mumbled, "I know. We can wait a year if you want."

"I will think about it," she said.

"I best be going. I need to start the paper work at the land office. I must think of our future and the future of our children. I hope you know to put the needs of our lineage ahead of ourselves."

"It is a big step, Phillip. I am not sure of my feelings for you," she said as tears stood in her eyes.

"My love for you is strong enough for the both of us. You will grow to love me," he said.

"I don't know..."

Phillip rose and kissed her on the forehead. "I know and that is all that matters," he said as he left the room.

Chapter 17

The smell of snow was in the air in the high altitude above timberline. Timothy could hardly believe that this was his third Christmas away from home. The outlaws never trusted him to go down the mountain with them on their raids, so they left him with Victoria at the cave. When the men were around, she barely spoke to him.

He knew that he was alive now only because of her pleading. They were set on killing him but she wouldn't hear of it. She called him her slave boy. He didn't like the term but it was the truth. He labored sunup to sundown for her. She had been harsh in her orders at first, but as he grew older, she had a change of attitude toward him.

He dropped an armload of wood in the entrance of the cave and stacked it neatly next to the grub box. The gang would soon return with staples of coffee, sugar, flour, beans, and crackers. Victoria sauntered to the entrance with the ever-present shotgun at her side. He looked in her direction and smiled. "It will be Christmas soon," he said.

"What are you going to get for me?" she asked.

He looked at the woman, noticing her piercing brown eyes.

Hard lines framed her mouth and the corners of her eyes. *Yes, 'hard' describes her well,* he thought.

She was strong, even though she was scrawny. Her neck was a match for the wild Tom turkey's that he had shot for supper. Streaks of white mingled with the thinning black hair pulled back in a bun at the nape of her neck. She was neither pretty nor ugly to him. She was just Victoria, his jailer.

"I brought you firewood. Merry Christmas!" he laughed.

She leaned the gun against the wall of the cave and took a necklace from around her neck. She fingered the long key that dangled from the chain as she paused in front of him. Quickly she slid the key into the lock of the leg iron around his right ankle. He watched in amazement as the heavy chain fell away from him. She slid her hands up his chest and lunged at him. Wrapping her arms around his neck, she kissed him hard on the mouth. "Timothy, I want ..." she began.

"No, you are old enough to be my mother," he yelled as he pulled away.

She shrieked. "Mother...I am not your mother. Do you think you are something special?"

He ran from the cave out into the open. Looking for cover, he ran down the draw among large rock formations, moving as quickly as he could without falling onto the rocky path. The shotgun blast sounded and struck a large boulder next to his shoulder.

He plunged into thick brush and took cover in the trees as he ran along the little stream from where he hauled water. Bullets pelted an outcropping of boulders above his head. He ran for his life. The wind picked up into a harsh blast and suddenly he was fighting to see through whirling snow. Visibility was impossible. *If I can't see the trees, then she can't see me.*

He took comfort in the thought and stumbled through the forest from tree to tree like a blind man. The blizzard conditions continued through the day and into the night. He kept moving even though the shots ceased. He had to keep moving or he would freeze to death. It was pitch black when the wind and snow stopped.

Timothy turned to see if his tracks were visible. The gang would be home soon and he knew he would be dead if they could track him. He was surprised to see that the blizzard had swept away all indications of his passing by. The only tracks showing were the ones he made since the wind stopped. Maybe he had a chance.

He heard a sound in the distance. It was some sort of music. *Could it be the gang?* he wondered. Silently he trudged through the deep snow and spotted the glowing of a campfire. *Indians don't play that kind of music.* Only one mule was tied to the tree next to the campfire. He didn't recognize it as belonging to any of the outlaws. The music rang out loud and clear. It was a Christmas carol but Timothy couldn't remember the name of it.

He peered through the brush and saw a small man bundled in a sheepskin coat sitting on a fallen log next to the fire. He held a thin silver box to his mouth and breathed in and out, making the music.

The man took the instrument from his mouth, slapped it against his thigh, and shouted loudly, "Hello, friend, welcome to my camp. My name is Henry and this is my harmonica. Are you hungry?"

Timothy stood frozen to the spot.

"Come on, boy. No one is going to find you out here. You must be half frozen by now," Henry said.

Timothy shuffled into the camp and stood next to the fire. "Thank you, sir."

"Call me 'Henry'. Take this cup of coffee. It will warm your innards," he said.

Drinking the warm liquid helped him feel human again. "Why are you out here at this time of year?" Timothy ventured.

"I could ask you the same thing, but I will answer you instead. I am here on a mission. We will talk more after you have something to eat and get thoroughly warmed up," he said.

Timothy ate his fill of beans and bacon. Hot coffee and fire were a welcome relief. "Thank you, Henry. You have been so kind."

His host laughed heartily and played loudly on the harmonica. He paused to sing the lyrics equally loud and with much gusto and minimum vocal skill. Timothy laughed at the energy the man possessed.

He wondered how old the man was. He seemed to be older than his pa but he had never seen anyone with that much enthusiasm before.

He stood shorter than Timothy by about four to six inches. His legs were long and his waist was high. He wore a cap of rabbit skin that had flaps that covered his ears and tied under his ample chin. He was not fat, but he was not thin either. His laughter came easily. Timothy watched him in wonder. *What kind of man is this?*

Henry took the harmonica from his lips and leaned close to Timothy. His small bright blue eyes were wide in excitement. "I am here to tell you that you need to go back to Boston. Your papa is dying and he needs to see you."

"How do you know this?" Timothy asked.

"You will know more tomorrow. Now it is time for you to get some sleep," he said.

Henry led Timothy to a buffalo hide next to the fire. Without a word, Timothy lay down. He watched the man until his eyes grew heavy. He was so tired that he slept through the night.

Timothy awoke to the sound of branches snapping. He sat up and saw Henry breaking a branch over his knee before he fed the fire. "Answer my question," he said.

Henry put his finger to his lips. "Shhhh…"

"Hello the camp!" came a shout from the woods.

"Welcome friends," Henry replied as he stood between the fire and Timothy.

Timothy's heart leaped into his throat as he saw all of the outlaws file into the camp and sit on the log.

"Help yourself to the coffee. There is plenty," said Henry.

"Don't mind if we do," said the Old Man.

Henry grinned and asked, "What are you fellers doing out in this kind of weather? Don't you have a place to hang your hat?"

"My boy run off last night. I am afraid he might be frozen to death somewhere out here. My friends volunteered to help me find him and bring him home."

Henry took a sip of coffee. "…Do tell?"

Timothy was frozen to the spot. It didn't appear that any of the men had spotted him. He dared not move a muscle.

"Have you seen him, mister?"

"Nope, I can't say as I saw your son. I've been doing my best to weather the storm. I am way off my stompin' grounds. This isn't my trapping area. I got turned onto this place in the storm. Hopefully, I can leave shortly. I think the weather is goin' to hold for awhile. Do you?" asked Henry.

Timothy eyed each of the men. They seemed to look straight through him. His head began to throb.

"Thank ya fer the coffee. If you see the boy, tell him to high tail it home."

"I will," Henry laughed as he began playing 'Old Suzanna' on the harmonica.

The men mounted their horses and left.

Henry played many verses of the song, took the instrument from his lips, and smacked it against his thigh. He looked at Timothy and said, "Remember, you have to go home to your papa. He has something he needs to tell you."

Timothy opened his mouth to answer, but Henry was gone.

Chapter 18

Gracie stood at the fireplace after placing another log on the fire. She sat in her rocker and placed her hands on her swollen stomach. It wouldn't be long before her second child would enter her life. It was almost Christmas. She had most everything ready for little Wayne. She had knitted new socks and a new warm sweater for him.

Phillip purchased him a little carved horse. She reached for it and found a bit of brown paper to wrap it in. The little horse had been painted white. *It reminds me of Chowder.* It had been a long time since she had allowed herself to think of Timothy and his horse. *I wonder whatever became of them.* She finished wrapping the gift and tied one of her blue hair ribbons around it. Wayne would love opening the pretty package.

He was two years old now and would enjoy Christmas. He was her joy. His light brown hair and sweet brown eyes were a perfect fit for his little body. She knew he was the most intelligent child she had ever known. He was protective of his mother. She sighed and stood. She placed the gift under the Christmas tree. Its fragrance filled the room. Tonight she planned to pop some corn and thread it onto some string to decorate the tree.

Wayne would love that. Hopefully, Phillip wouldn't mind. He had tried to be more cheerful lately. It was Christmas. He would be cheerful.

"Mama, did it snow? Can we play?" Wayne lisped.

"Soon, precious…it will snow by Christmas." She laughed as she picked up her son.

He snuggled into her arms and wrapped little arms around her neck. "I wuv you, Mama."

"I love you, Wayne," she said as she rocked him in the squeaky rocking chair.

The door creaked open and Phillip quietly slipped inside. He smiled widely and put his finger to his lips, urging her to silence. Gracie looked down at her sleeping son, then looked up into the face of her husband.

He placed an armload of wood beside the fireplace and stepped next to her. He touched the top of her head with his large, rough hand and traced the contour of her cheek with his fingers. "Take him on to bed and I will help you with Christmas things."

She nodded and accepted his help in getting to her feet. The unborn baby was certainly making getting around more difficult. "Thank you," she whispered as she lay the toddler down.

Phillip watched her with his child. *She is a very good mother and a fine looking woman.* He noted her shoulder-length hair curling around her pale face. As he enfolded her into his arms, he snagged a lock of the shiny black hair and pulled it down straight.

It reached to the middle of her back before it slipped from his fingers and bounced back to shoulder length.

She looked into his face and grinned. Her eyes were sky blue tonight and danced in the light of the fire in the hearth. "This is going to be a good Christmas. Thank you, Phillip."

"How are you feeling today, little Mama?"

Gracie put her head on his shoulder. "I think our baby will come before the New Year dawns."

"I suspected as much. We do have Christmas, though. You really should rest before the wee one arrives. What do you need done?"

"I was going to pop some corn and string it to put on the tree," she said.

Phillip led her to the rocker. "You sit here. I think I can pop the corn."

She watched as he popped the corn over the fire in the fireplace. When he finished, she handed him a ball of yarn from her latest project. "I need to find my big darning needle so that the yarn will fit through the eye." She threaded the needle with the yarn and handed it to Phillip.

"This should be fun," he said.

"Just push the needle through each piece of the popped corn. You can let some of the bright red thread show between them so that it is more colorful."

After the pan of popped corn was strung onto the yarn, Gracie yawned sleepily. The gesture was not lost on Phillip.

He said, "Wayne will love this. Let me put it on the tree while you watch."

"You are most kind, dear Phillip."

"I wished to keep bad news from you, my dear," Phillip said.

Gracie gulped.

"I'm all in, Gracie. The farm isn't producing enough for us to survive. I don't want to take hand-outs from your folks anymore."

"They don't mind," she said.

"Please hear me out."

She nodded.

"I have heard of work that I know I can do. It involves driving a team of mules through Death Valley, California. I am determined to do this."

"Death Valley...is it far away?"

"The pay is one hundred dollars a month each for the mule skinner and the swamper. We could be rich!"

"Are you sure they pay that much?" Gracie asked.

"They do because it takes skill to drive twenty mules through the desert."

"It sounds difficult."

He could see that she was uncomfortable with the decision. "I need you do go with me."

"Me?"

"You can be the swamper. All you have to do is work the brake and throw rocks at the mules that are not alert."

"How can I do that with my babies to care for?"

"You have to. Your folks can take care of the babies. We will send them money for their efforts."

"I can't leave my babies!"

"You have to. We owe the bank and everyone else."

"Who else?" The frown on Gracie's brow was pronounced.

"All right, I tried making some money by gambling."

"Gambling, how could you?" she croaked in a loud whisper.

"You have to work with me to help me pay my debts. The subject is closed."

"I simply cannot leave a nursing baby," Gracie said quietly.

"Bring it with you, but you must hide it."

"Why would I hide my own child?"

"They only hire unmarried men," he said.

"What?"

"You will have to cut off your hair and wear overalls and big shirts. We will figure out the baby thing when we come to it."

Gracie stood slowly and paced across the floor, wringing her hands. "I don't know…I don't want to leave little Wayne." Tears slipped down her cheeks.

"We have to make this work or the men will kill me," Phillip said urgently.

She shrugged. "No, I couldn't…"

"After you have this baby, we will set out to California. I have already sent a telegram and they want us."

"It sounds very dangerous."

"No one has died doing this in the three years they have been in operation. We will do fine."

"How long will we be away?"

"If I send payments to the men and we pay your folks, we should be home in ten months."

"That is almost a year! Wayne won't even know me!"

"You will have the rest of your life to reacquaint yourself with Wayne."

"Phillip, you are breaking my heart. Please, don't make me go."

"This is what you have to do. You are my wife. You do not have a choice."

She stumbled to the big feather bed. Her eyes were heavy and sleep was fitful. Her dreams were of her sweet little boy crying for his mama. She dreamed that she ran through deep sand trying to reach Wayne while he called out for her. Just as she touched his pudgy little hand, Phillip pulled her away.

She awoke. "Oh God, I can't leave Wayne. How can I leave him?" She swallowed sobs while Phillip snored loudly.

She arose, went to the fireplace, and stoked the fire, bringing it back to life. Placing a small log on the fire, she sat in her sturdy rocker and watched the fire lick the edges of the fresh wood. She felt that her heart had been taken from her chest. Her mind was full of conflict.

She knew that she had to obey her husband, yet love for her child was stronger. *I can't help it. I love Wayne more than Phillip. Forgive me, God.* She fidgeted in her chair. *It is so unfair for Phillip to ask me to do this. How does he know I can do this work? Why did he gamble? Do I have to pay for his sins?*

The sound of snoring in the adjoining room infuriated her. *How can you sleep like a baby while my heart is broken?* Wayne whimpered. Gracie moved carefully and found him in the bed next to his father. He put his chubby arms around her neck and held on tightly as she carried him to the rocker. His head rested on her shoulder while his breath washed over her cheek. Fresh tears streamed down her cheeks. She rocked slowly and pondered her predicament. She knew that if she went to her mother and father, they would send her home to her husband. There was no answer for her.

As the fingers of light filtered through the cloudy night, she realized that she had no choice but to go to California with her husband. Maybe the debt would be paid sooner than Phillip thought. She would see to it that they were frugal with their spending. She determined to get those debts paid as soon as possible. *At least I will have my new baby with me. I don't know how I will hide him. God, you will have to help me.*

Phillip awoke at sunup and sprang to his feet. "Merry Christmas, Gracie! Wake that little boy up. He needs to see the tree."

Wayne woke at the sound of his father's voice. "Tree, tree!" he said as he pointed to the small tree in the middle of the table.

Gracie dragged her red eyes to the festive greenery. Somehow, the beauty diminished markedly after the talk Phillip had with her.

Wayne danced and clapped his hands. "Pretty tree...pretty tree."

"It's a Christmas tree, sweetheart." Gracie said.

"Kissmass tree..." he said pointing to the evergreen.

*****

Wayne's chubby arms clung tightly to Gracie's neck. He wrapped his legs around her waist and held on. Phillip pulled on him and his grip tightened. Gracie didn't want to let go of her child, either. After much struggle, Wayne was in his grandfather's arms. Gracie's mother kissed her on the cheek as she placed the newborn baby girl into her arms. Gracie wrapped a shawl around herself and the baby, creating a sling. The little one slept comfortably.

Wayne leaned forward, reaching out and crying, "Mama, me want mama!"

"Please, Phillip, I can't do this!" she cried.

"Hush. We have no choice," he said.

He pushed Gracie up to the wagon seat and handed her the baby.

She couldn't bear to look down at Wayne, even though she heard his loud wailing. She had never known such heartache before. Somehow she would be back. She had to come home to her son.

She cried every waking hour most of the way to the Harmony Borax works at the Furnace Creek Ranch in California. Two days before their arrival, she felt her spirit break inside of her. There were no tears left. She felt no emotion at all. The baby cried and she tended to her, but she possessed no feelings for her or Phillip.

Phillip grew concerned because she refused to name the child. He called her Hope because he knew in his heart that after running the mule teams, his luck would change. He looked at his young wife. She was looking poorly. Her cheeks were sunken as well as her eyes. He caught her eyes but they were lifeless, cold, icy blue. Although she said nothing to him, he knew that she judged him and held him with contempt. There was no hint of recognition, only resignation. *I will make it all up to her. She will thank me in the end.*

He poured a cup of strong coffee from the pot on the campfire.

"Gracie, have you thought of how you are going to hide the baby?" he asked.

She shrugged.

"Answer me! You might as well figure this out or you will never see Wayne again." His voice was threatening.

She wrapped the baby tightly to her body and buttoned on a large shirt. Grabbing a worn brown felt hat, she smashed it down on her head. She tried to tuck in the wispy curls, but some of them escaped.

Phillip yanked the hat off her head and drew his knife from the sheath in his boot. He sliced off each curl, one by one down to her scalp and burned each of them in the campfire. It left her practically bald. She touched her head and felt the ravages of the knife. He pulled the hat down almost past her ears. "You are going to have to keep your face and hands dirty so no one will guess that you are a woman."

She shrugged. It was humiliating for him to eliminate all of her hair, but he had already taken so much from her, it didn't matter. She slumped as she sat on a tree stump next to their campfire. The baby whimpered and she adjusted Hope to nurse.

"Tomorrow we arrive at the borax mine. We will find out when we take our first load then," he said. "You are gonna have to see to it that Hope doesn't make a noise when we are not alone."

"How am I supposed to do that?" she cried.

"How should I know? Do your mothering magic or give her whiskey. I don't care. I don't know why you brought her with you," he snarled.

She looked at the small baby at her breast. *How on earth am I going to do this?*

Chapter 19

"This is your team. You and your swamper must know all of them by name. This bunch is easier than most to remember because most of the twenty are named for the twelve disciples. This head-strong one is Peter. You will always find these two together, so they are called James and Matthew. This is Andrew and this one is Barthomew. Nathaniel and Thomas have to be pushed a little. The others are Lainey, Bossy, Buddy..."

The names rattled easily off the tongue of the man. Gracie couldn't imagine how twenty mules worked together in a team. Now she had to help drive them. What was Phillip thinking?

"You must hitch them exactly the same each day. These two are the most intelligent. They are the leaders. The pointers, sixes, and eights jump the chain when you come to a bend in the road. They pull counter to the direction you are aimin' at. In doing so, it causes the wagon to turn. The two big horses are the wheelers. The driver rides on the nigh wheeler. We use the horses for strength. The mules are capable of learning to jump the chain where horses refuse."

"Nigh wheeler?" Phillip asked.

"Left-handed horse next to the wagon...you can operate the brake on the front wagon from the back of the nigh wheeler. Remember, you are pulling a load of sixty thousand pounds counting your water for the dry camps. You had better treat these beasts like kings. Make sure they get plenty of feed and water."

"They can only do about eighteen miles per day. We have some stops closer than that because of the terrain. We have stations for you to stop at. You will find a large corral and feed and hay at each one. Each stop has a small shelter for the skinner and swamper. You will run onto a returning team every four days on the trail to Mojave. After you unload at the drop off point, you go and purchase supplies for the stations and drop off a measure at each one. That is how these are supplied. In the stops where there is no water, you will have to use water from the water tank you take with you. Use it sparingly, because you will need it at the next dry hole. The whole turn around is 20 days for the 330 miles. You will not be allotted more than a day to get your supplies together so there will be no time for drinkin', gamblin', or chasin' skirts. You got my meanin'?" He looked at the dirty kid standing next to Phillip. "You sure he's up for the job?"

Phillip nodded, "Course. The kid is scrawny, but he is a hard worker. He don't say much, but he gets all of your meaning. He is good with animals and will be a good skinner."

Mr. Clay gave a small pencil chart of the mules' positions in their harnesses. Gracie took it and gave a slight nod. *Thank You, God, for this small favor.* She blinked quickly to keep tears from forming. She worried about Hope. The baby hadn't moved a muscle since she caught Phillip putting whiskey in a large dropper and squirting it down Hope's throat. The poor infant screamed loudly. Gracie tried to ease the pain in the little throat by allowing her to nurse a bit more. Hope slept immediately. Gracie had tied her tightly to her midsection and put on the loose fitting shirt and overalls. She slammed her hat over her ugly head. Things couldn't get any worse as far as Gracie was concerned. She kept her eyes on the paper, attempting to memorize the names and where they were positioned in the team. She cursed.

Phillip stood stock still. He slapped her across the face.

Mr. Clay watched with a narrowing gaze.

Phillip tipped his head toward Gracie as he spoke to Mr. Clay, "No mere skinner will curse me as long as I am boss. I won't abide it."

Gracie spat blood near his foot. "No sir, I reckon you won't."

His face burned hotter than the wind that scorched the barren earth of the street where they stood. "We best rest up tonight. Morning will come sooner than we expect. Goodnight, Mr. Clay," he said.

"Goodnight."

Chapter 20

Boston hadn't changed a bit since he had left those five years ago. His skin crawled when he saw the barn where so much of his earlier life was plagued with fear. It occurred to him that he hadn't lived the life of a free man many of those years since he left. He determined to shake off the chains of slavery for good and be sure that it never happened again. He didn't know why he obeyed the strange little man named Henry, but he felt compelled to do his bidding, especially when he discovered a few golden coins in his saddlebag.

The door opened easily as he walked into his old home. The place looked much the same. He was surprised that there were no whiskey bottles strewn across the floor. His eyes fell on a large black book in the middle of the rough old dinner table. A *Bible?* He turned his eyes toward the cot. The face of the man on the cot was that of his father, but the body was much different. The man had a huge, distended stomach. His breathing was labored. A doctor entered the room and introduced himself to Timothy. "I am Dr. Swanson. You must be Timothy, the son?"

"Yes sir," he said.

"Your father has a condition of the liver that causes much swelling. Much of the water of his body is contained in his belly. "

Timothy studied the form of his father. His skin was yellowed and the muscles sagged. There were deep wrinkles around his mouth. He came closer and Cecil's eyes opened. Timothy saw that the chocolate-brown eyes were clear and sober. Tears stood in the corners and spilled down the hard, wrinkled cheeks.

"Timothy, are you a dream or are you really here?" Cecil whispered.

"I am here. You don't look so good."

"I am dying, son. I am glad you are here."

Timothy shifted from one foot to the other.

"Son, I made my peace with God. I want to make peace with you. I am telling you that I am sorry for how I always treated you. There really was no good excuse. You were always a good boy. You didn't deserve the things I did to you."

Timothy studied the face. It was not the face of rage that he knew. This was a man he had never seen before. The door creaked and Timothy turned to see Uncle John entering the room. John grabbed the boy and held him close.

"You are a sight for sore eyes, Tim. I am so glad you came."

Timothy breathed in the scent of the uncle who had rescued him. It brought him comfort. "I am glad I am here, too," he said.

"Your father has been calling for you. It is good that you are here."

Timothy knelt next to Cecil and put his hand on the withered chest.

"Papa, I forgave you a long time ago. I have just been so afraid of you that I didn't come home."

"You had every right to be afraid," Cecil said and finished with a round of raspy coughing.

"The 'death rattle' is in his chest, boy. It won't be long now," Dr. Swanson said quietly.

"I know I am close to the end," Cecil said.

Timothy leaned close to the man to hear the barely audible words. "Tim, God found me and He changed me."

Timothy could hardly believe the words whispered from his father's lips. "I found God, too," he said softly.

Cecil nodded slightly and took two gulping breaths. His breathing stopped and the doctor listened for a heartbeat.

"He is gone, Timothy," Dr. Swanson declared.

Timothy stood looking at the man. *I wish you had known God when I was young, Papa.*

"Tim, come to my place and stay with me for a bit. Doctor, thank you for all that you have done for Cecil. You have been most kind."

Dr. Swanson placed the stethoscope into his bag. "I will tell the undertaker to come on my way to my house."

"Thank you, doc."

"Come on, Tim. You need something to eat. We will tend to his burial tomorrow morning." John said.

The two left the room and Timothy cast a look at the peaceful face of his father. "Rest in peace, Papa," he said.

Chapter 21

John Forrester watched the scenery pass from his seat on the train. He was glad to go somewhere new to live. He looked at his nephew and grinned. Timothy had grown up in the five years he had been gone. When he left, he was a skinny little thirteen-year-old. Now he was eighteen and had seen more things than his old uncle had in his life. The boy was brave. It was hard to believe the things that Timothy had suffered.

"Uncle John, I hope it wasn't too hard on you to leave Boston," Timothy said quietly.

John rubbed his chin and grinned. "Truth be told, Tim, I am tired of being alone. Since you are the adventurous type, I am bound to follow wherever you go."

"I know you have been to Trinidad, Colorado before. I saw you and Papa get off the train."

"That is why you disappeared from the ranch you worked at?"

"I couldn't let Papa ...get to me," Timothy said.

John nodded. "I hear 'ya. The family you worked for seemed to be good people."

"I have to go back and explain what happened. I would like to stay there for awhile until we decide where we want to live."

"Sounds like a good plan to me."

*****

The men enjoyed getting reacquainted on the long trip to Colorado. It was needful time for both of them. They shared the sorrow of loving the man who had squandered his life with bitterness and hatred. They rejoiced that in his later years he had found peace that only God could have brought into the devastated soul. They enjoyed one another's company and were glad to begin a new life in a new place.

The train screeched to a stop at the depot in Trinidad at early evening. Each disembarked from the train with a valise in his hand. John waited on the platform until a large wooden crate was unloaded from the boxcar. It held all of his blacksmith tools as well as carpentry tools of Cecil's. These would be used for his livelihood in this new adventure. He made arrangements with the station master to allow the box to be stored until he found a permanent place to reside. The two walked directly to the hotel to get a room.

Timothy could hardly believe the growth that the town had experienced since he had left. Things were progressing nicely. He determined that he would visit with all the members of the Young family tomorrow. They would be glad to see Uncle John again since he had met with them when Papa and he came to find him.

I wonder if Gracie is still here. She is probably married by now. Still, I have to see whatever became of her.

The two freshened up and went into the dining room for a bite to eat. As they sat waiting for the dinner of roasted beef, a tall, blond-haired man seated himself at a nearby table.

"Elmer, is that you?" Timothy asked.

"I declare! Timothy, where have you been?"

"That is a long story. Have you met my Uncle John?"

"Yes, I have had the pleasure. How are you, John? I see that you found that run-away nephew," he laughed.

"Sit with us, Elmer."

Elmer pushed back from his table and sat with Timothy and John. "Where is Cecil?"

"He passed away last month," Timothy said.

"Sorry to hear that."

"He took sick right after we were here three years ago. It was an ugly death. He is at peace now," John said.

"What did he die from?" Elmer asked.

"It was a disease in his liver...from the drinking."

"That is a hard way to die. I am sorry for all of you."

They sat in silence as the waitress brought steaming plates of food to the table.

"Millie, how did you know what I wanted?" Elmer asked, grinning.

"Why wouldn't I know? You eat here every time roast beef is the special." She said.

Elmer shook his head and spread out his napkin. "You mind if we bless the food?" he asked.

They bowed their heads and Elmer proceeded with a short prayer and a loud 'amen.'

Patrons of the restaurant eavesdropped on the jovial men eating together. Time after time the conversation was sprinkled with laughter. They spoke with gusto and animation. It was almost as entertaining as a school play. After much time had elapsed the three said their 'good-byes'.

"I will see you at Fred and Nan's house first thing in the morning," Elmer said as he left them.

*****

Timothy could hardly wait for the door to open. He looked down to see a sweet-faced five-year-old girl standing by the door. Elmer stood behind her.

"Hi. Uncle Elmer says to let you come inside," she said, grinning.

"Who might you be?" John asked.

"I am Rose Young," she smiled widely revealing the lack of two front teeth.

"Come on in. Nan and Fred are in the kitchen waiting for you," Elmer interjected.

The coziness of the large kitchen embraced John. He noted the large wood stove with a steaming kettle of beans on the back burner, loaves of bread sitting on the sideboard covered with large white dishtowels, and a large white enamel pot of coffee on the front of the stove. Fred stood and retrieved the coffee pot as Nan placed two more cups and saucers on the large, round, oak table.

"You boys will be wanting coffee, I am a thinkin'," Fred said indicating chairs for them to take.

Nan threw her arms around Timothy and kissed him on the cheek. "I never quit praying for you, Timothy. You are dear to my heart."

"I needed every one of those prayers, Miss Nan," Timothy said quietly.

"We are glad to have you home," Fred said, and turning to John, "Will you two be settling here?"

"That is the plan," John answered.

Nan walked to the doorway and spoke loudly, "Sally... June...it is time to get to school. Make sure that Rose doesn't forget her to take her lessons with her."

Nan sat and took a sip of her cup of coffee that was heavily laced with sugar and cream. "I don't know how you men can abide this stuff without doctoring it up with at least some sugar."

"We will get straightened out after we get married," Elmer said, laughing.

"Are you planning on getting married?" John asked.

"Don't you know that is why the Good Lord put us on this earth? We are supposed to get married and do the bidding of womenfolk," he said.

"Oh dear me," Nan said. "To think that I have wasted all these years not getting Fred to do 'my bidding'."

Fred pulled her chair close to his and kissed her on the forehead.

"Of course I do your bidding, Nannygirl. We just don't call it that."

"I can see that Elmer might need some good polishing, but me and John....we are just fine," Tim said playfully.

"Spoken like a confirmed, eternal bachelor," Elmer answered in kind.

"Speaking of marriage, is Gracie married?" Timothy asked.

Fred nodded. "Yes, close to three years now. She has two young'uns.Her papa said that she had to leave the oldest one with them to work with her husband driving mule teams in California."

"Leave her child?" Timothy asked in disbelief.

Nan added, "She has a new-born that she took with her. I don't know what Phillip Masters was thinking."

"That is who she married?"

"I am afraid that it is not a good fit. He is given to drink and gambling," Nan said.

"Remember to be gracious, Nan. We don't know their marriage," Fred warned.

Timothy frowned. *It must have been hard to leave her child behind.*

"Forgive me for gossiping. I am just so upset about her having to be a swamper on the mule team. I am beside myself with anger. Emily Randall is not a bit happy, either. Clyde thought that Phillip was made of better stuff than that, but he was wrong."

"Nan!" Fred exclaimed.

Nan shook her head and said, "I am sorry. With this situation, it is hard to keep my opinions to myself. Forgive me, please."

Timothy felt the heat on his neck. *I wish I could get my hands on that man!*

John broke the spell. "Fred, do you think that there is much call in this area for carpenters or smithys? I have tools and skills in those professions."

"We always have need for good blacksmiths. In fact, I have a shed next to the house that you could use for your shop," Fred said.

"Thank you so much. I don't know how to pass the time without working with my hands. It will be good to start up again," John said excitedly.

"John, would you want to go to Ted and Mandy's spread with me? I want to see them before the day is over," Timothy said.

John pushed back his chair and stood. "Thank you for the coffee. It was very good to see you again," he said as he shook Fred's hand and nodded toward Nan.

*****

Miranda carried a full pail of water from the pump to the large kettle on the stove. Zachary trotted behind her as fast as his four-year-old legs would carry him. Timothy could tell by the wash on the clothesline that it was washday.

"Manda, you need help fetchin' some water?" he asked.

Miranda's face was wreathed in smiles. "Timothy, is that you? Oh my goodness! You have grown a foot taller!" she exclaimed.

"It has been a long time. I didn't mean to leave without saying anything. I just had to get away."

Miranda saw John standing next to one of Fred's horses. "Hello, John. You found him?"

"Actually, he came home in time to see Cecil before he died," John said.

"Your father died, then. I am sorry." She put her hand on his arm and gave it a little squeeze.

Zach wasn't used to being ignored. "Who are you?" he asked.

"I am Timothy. Who are you?"

"I am Zach Young. I am four years old."

"Well, I am pleased to meet you, Zach Young."

"You are funny," he said as he skipped to the house.

Timothy grinned at Miranda. "So this is the baby that made you so sick that we were afraid you were dying or something."

"The one and only," she said.

"Come on in and get some dinner."

"Maybe next time, Manda. Where is Ted?"

"He is in the far pasture. Do you remember where it is?"

"How could I ever forget this place? I am sure it is second only to heaven."

John and Timothy mounted the horses and bade Miranda and Zachary goodbye. They found Ted assisting a young cow in birthing her calf.

The calf stood on his wobbly legs and found the nourishment from his mother. Ted jogged to the men and gave Timothy a hearty hug.

"Timothy, you made it back. I can't tell you how many times you have been on my mind since you left."

"This place and your family have never been out of my mind, either," Timothy said.

"Do you boys need work? I got a' plenty to keep a dozen busy."

John shook Ted's hand and said, "I'm going to start up a blacksmith shop in town, but thank you anyhow."

"When do you want me to start?" Timothy asked.

Chapter 22

Sweat mingled with the hot urine that ran down Gracie's stomach. The stench was almost more than she could bear. The only thing worse was the terrible heat. *I am in hell. There is no way out of here.* Baby Hope was tied to the front of her so that she could nurse easily. Gracie kept the dreadful long-sleeved shirt on and unbuttoned it so that the tiny baby could get a breath of air and be shaded from the harsh sun. One of the drivers they met at the last station remarked that it would grow hotter. The hottest recorded temperature in Death Valley was one hundred sixty degrees. *The baby and I will both die if we make another trip.*

Gracie's face was wind-burned. She kept a large sombrero-style hat on to shade as much of her body as possible, but her face and neck were like red leather. Phillip was tanned as dark as the Indians that she saw along the trail. She picked up a sharp rock and lobbed it at Lainey. That mule was drifting off to sleep. It was her job to make sure all the mules were alert. Lainey started out of her daze and trudged on under the heavy weight.

This was the third trip back to Mojave and Phillip had gambled away all of the money except a few coins she had slipped from the bag before he went to the saloon. No money had been paid toward the debt he owed.

At this rate she would never get to go home to little Wayne.

The last trip had been the worst of the three they had traveled. When they came to the Wingate Pass where the mules jumped the chain, one of the mules came close to the edge of the cliff with his hoof. An avalanche of rock poured out from under him and he jumped sideways into his harness mate. The team spooked, but Phillip held them under control until the turn was completed. Gracie felt sorry for Old Peter because Phillip beat him unmercifully when the danger passed.

Tears dripped from her chin. The hot wind dried them into dirt streaks on her face. Phillip turned around and looked at her from the back of the big horse closest to the wagon on the left side. He frowned. She frowned back.

I have to get some more money so I can leave him. I am going home. I don't care what anyone thinks. I am done with living like this. I am a mother. The ticket master at the train depot said I needed $9.48 to get home.

She had counted out the coins to find that she only had $4.92 from her efforts to steal from Phillip each trip. She would get the rest this time. She couldn't do this again. She watched Phillip as he rode proudly on the back of the big horse.

I hate him. I have never hated anyone as much as I hate him.

As the day crawled to the arrival at Blackwater Well, the last station before they arrived in Mohave,

Gracie planned her movements for after Phillip got paid.

She puzzled as to how she would get another five dollars out from under Phillip's nose. He always made her go to the bath house and get cleaned up while he went gambling. Even though she needed the bath, maybe she would go straight to the train station. They might not let her on the train with the residue from the baby diapers clinging to her skin. She would bathe but it would have to be cut short so that she could leave undetected by Phillip.

"Are you gonna help me or what?" Phillip screamed.

She shook out of her planning and realized that they were at Blackwater. It was a 'dry station' and they had to water the mules from the tank that the previous team had left behind for them to use. Phillip had her release the valve to fill the water troughs. After that, she helped unharness all eighteen mules and the horses, and pitch hay for them while Phillip managed the feed. After the mules and horses were cared for, she cooked supper while Phillip rested. She wondered how the jobs were divided on the other teams. It didn't matter. She was supposed to obey her husband no matter what he said. That is what her mother always told her.

I don't care what Mama says, I am leaving and never coming back to Phillip. I will learn to make my own living...somehow.

She grew quiet and retreated into her thoughts. There were very few opportunities for women.

If her dad wouldn't let her live with them, she and her children would have to fend for themselves. If she divorced Phillip, no school board would hire her to teach the school children. If she simply left him, it might be the same result. She had small children to think of. *If Papa knew that Phillip wasn't paying his debts and gambled all the money away, he might let me stay. God, I don't know what I am going to do.*

*****

Phillip and Gracie awakened early the last day of the route. Baby Hope was listless, as usual. Gracie put her in the sling and looked at her carefully. The infant caught the look and her little blue eyes shined in anticipation. "Hope, this will be a hard day. I haven't acted like it, but I do love you."

The little one cooed and gave a bright little smile.

"You best keep that one quiet else I will slam her head on the wagon wheel and kill her," Phillip growled.

Gracie ducked her head.

"Cover up that ugly head of yours, woman. You look worse than a blister on an old maid's foot!"

Gracie slammed the sombrero onto her head and swore under her breath. She tied the baby snugly to her body and hitched the mules in specific order.

She gave old Peter a gentle pat as she put him in his harness.

"Be good, Peter. Don't be scared when we come to the pass. You will do fine."

"Are you about ready to move out or are you gonna gab at those fool mules all day!" he yelled.

She scurried up to her perch on the second wagon next to the brake. She looked down at Hope and kissed her on the cheek. "Mama does love you, baby girl. I won't let him touch you."

Phillip cracked the twenty-five-foot whip over the heads of the mule team and they began the long tiresome day. When they arrived at the noon stop, Gracie led the mules in harness to the water troughs while Phillip gave them feed and hay. Gracie built a fire and cooked a quick meal of bacon and corn mush. It was filling, but she was tired of trail food. Phillip grunted when he saw it. "Get me the whiskey," he said.

"The boss-man said we wouldn't get paid if you had whiskey on your breath when we get to town, so I didn't bring it from the last stop." she said.

Before she could blink, a slap landed on her jaw. It sent her sprawling across the floor of the crude shed. Her whole face ached and one of her teeth felt loose. She sat up and checked on the baby. At least she managed to land on her back so that she wouldn't crush Hope. Gracie didn't look at Phillip. She was afraid he would see the hate in her eyes and know that something was afoot.

She cleaned up the mess from dinner and hitched the mules to the wagons. They pulled into Mohave just as the sun went down. The boss man, Mr. Clay, looked over the load and the stock. He took note of the swollen red print on Gracie's tired face. He dropped the small bag of gold coins as she reached her hand for it. She got on her knees to pick the coins that scattered on the floor. He knelt beside her to assist and whispered in her ear, "You best make a get-away, Miss, if you want to live."

She blinked quickly. The man knew she was a woman. "I...uh...yes, sir," she stammered. She took the bag and looked at Phillip. He hadn't heard the exchange. She slipped her forefinger into the opening of the bag and took hold of a ten dollar gold piece. She put it in the baby's diaper front. Phillip wouldn't look there.

"Howdy, Mr. Clay. How come you are paying us in gold coin this time?" Phillip asked.

"I knew you would be here after the banks closed and might need your pay before morning," he said.

He looked intently into Gracie's eyes and gave a slight nod. While Phillip counted out the money in his pouch, Gracie mouthed the words, 'thank you' to the man.

Mr. Clay watched the woman with interest. The baby squirmed and his suspicions were confirmed. He handed her a note as he passed her and began a conversation with Phillip.

She hurriedly opened the note.

*****

I will detain him as long as possible. Go get a train and take all of your pay with you. I have hired some men to hold him up for awhile.

She looked back and saw Mr. Clay talking with Phillip. Two men came up to them and yelled at Phillip. Before Gracie knew what was going on, Phillip was involved in a fist fight with one of the men.

She took off running for the train depot. Her oversized boots pounded the ground and slowed her progress. She strained with every ounce of strength that was left in her body. Hope whimpered at being jostled so violently. Finally, she saw the train depot and found the ticket master's window.

"I need a ticket for Colorado," she gasped.

"Where abouts in Colorado?"

"Trinidad...please hurry."

"The train leaves in eight minutes. That will be nine dollars and eighty two cents."

She reached into the little bag and gave him a gold piece. He looked at it carefully and handed her a ticket. "You might want to sit close to the door. Decent folks frown on people who don't bathe."

"Thank you, sir," she said as she ran for the train.

She sat close to the door of the next to last passenger car and peered out the window toward the wagon station. Phillip was not running down the road to the train. She held her breath...waiting.

She heard several people coughing lightly and looked up. A couple of cowboys were frowning at her. They got out of their seats and moved as far from her as humanly possible. One of them looked back at her and said, "Hey kid, didn't your ma ever tell you to take a bath? You smell ripe!"

Gracie blushed to her toes. These people didn't know her. Tears threatened. She held them back. *It doesn't matter. I will never have to see them again.* The train lurched forward as the sun tipped onto the horizon.

She heard someone screaming in the street. "Gracie, get yourself off that blamed old train! If you don't, I am gonna catch you and kill you!"

She bit her lip as she saw him lunge toward the train. His foot landed on the step of the last passenger car. He ran down the aisle toward the car where she sat. Blood poured from his broken nose and busted lip. He waved his large Colt .45 as he progressed quickly toward her. Suddenly, the porter grabbed him by the arm.

"Put the gun away!"

"You gonna make me?"

The porter held his grip while a male passenger reached for the gun.

"Dad blame it! I come fer my woman!"

He wrenched away from the porter and lunged for the platform of the next car.

She stood and looked out the door, waiting for him to shoot her. She heard a loud scream with many profanities.

The train picked up speed. She stood motionless as she saw him crumpled on the tracks. His legs were severed. Blood flowed like a river. People gathered to look at him. A man pulled him off the tracks and rifled through his pockets. He found the small bag of gold and took it, leaving the man to bleed in the ditch.

Chapter 23

She stumbled to her seat and sat staring out the window, watching the landscape turn dark. She had to get her wits about her. The baby cried. Everything had happened so quickly. *Did Phillip die?* The baby continued its crying and passengers in the car looked back at her, startled.

A big man stomped up to her seat and yelled, "Where did you get that baby? Who did you steal it from?"

She stuck out her chin and answered, "Hope is my child. I am her mother!"

"Likely story," he sniffed.

A plain-looking woman got up from the front of the car and approached Gracie. She covered her nose and mouth with her handkerchief, but spoke kindly. "Little mother, if you like I will let you use my sleeping berth on your trip. You look awful tired."

Tears sprang into Gracie's eyes. "Why would you do that for me?"

"You remind me of myself when I was your age. Please, I will show you where it is."

Gracie followed the woman to a lower sleeping berth. It had a curtain to pull across it. She put her hand on Gracie's arm and said, "I have an extra dress in my bag. It is only a work dress, but it is clean. I think it will come close to fitting. Would that be all right?"

"Oh Ma'am, I am too dirty to put on anything clean."

"I will get the porter to bring you a wash basin and some rags and soap. I am sure there are towels to use for diapers, also. Don't worry; I will take care of everything. Go ahead and get into the sleeping berth."

Within the hour, the woman returned with the dress. A porter carried a large porcelain bowl and water pitcher. The porter handed her the bowl and said, "Ma'am, I will bring you another pitcher of water in a bit. The baby wants a bath too, no doubt."

"Thank you."

" Let me help you give the baby a bath. Did you say her name was Hope?"

"Yes, she is Hope. What is your name? Why are you being so kind?" Gracie asked.

The woman smiled widely. "My name is Mary Dewey. I am a preacher."

Air whistled through Gracie's teeth. "A woman preacher?"

"The reason I am doing this is because Jesus said that we are supposed to act as His hands to those who are in need. You looked to be someone with real needs.

I couldn't claim to belong to Him if I neglected you in any way. I am doing this because I love Him, and because I love Him, I love you also. What is your name, dear?"

"I am Gracie."

"I am glad to be of service to you and Hope, Gracie."

A large lump stuck in Gracie's throat and she was unable to answer.

Mary took the child and made quick work of the bath. She chuckled when she found the gold piece. "We better not tell anyone about the baby who laid a golden coin or we might be in trouble here."

Gracie grinned. "I knew he wouldn't look in a dirty diaper for the money," she said.

Mary bundled the baby in a large old tablecloth that the porter had found for her.

"Why don't I rock this baby while you take your own bath?"

"Thank you," she said as she watched Mary retreat to the passenger car to tend to Hope.

The porter arrived with another pitcher. He emptied the basin into the first pitcher and tossed the dirty water onto the tracks by way of the back door.

Finally alone, Gracie plunged her weathered hands into the clean, warm water. The slippery lye soap sent up a pleasing fragrance to her nostrils. She dipped the top of her head into the basin and lathered up the stubs of hair on her head. The water turned black.

She rinsed with some of the water remaining in the pitcher. She took the rag, lathered it up and scrubbed her stomach. It felt good to get the stench of leaky diapers off of her. She was amazed at the grime in the bottom of the basin. She was equally amazed at the feeling of clean on her skin. She slipped the soft old dress over her head. It made her feel like her old self.

A large lump formed in her throat as she thought of the trauma she had experienced on this very day. *Thank you, God, for helping me get away.*

She rubbed salty tears from her eyes as she thought of Phillip and how he had gone wrong. Her stomach lurched at the memory of the flowing blood.

Shaking her head to clear her thoughts, she opened the privacy curtains and stepped into the aisle. Finding her way to the passenger car, she sat next to Mary Dewey. Hope stretched her baby arms and wiggled happily in Mary's lap. *Poor baby has always been so confined...until now.*

Mary looked up into the tired blue eyes. "Go ahead and go to sleep in the sleeping berth. When Hope goes to sleep, I will put her in there with you. She will want to eat before too long, but you may as well get some rest while she is feeling so playful."

"Thank you...again," Gracie said as she slipped down the aisle and climbed into the sleeping booth.

How had the boss figured out that I was a woman? Why did he help me? What did I do to mess Phillip up like that? If only I had been a better wife.

Her mind tormented her before she drifted off to get some much-needed sleep.

*****

Mary placed the baby next to the sleeping woman. The child nuzzled her mother hungrily. Gracie opened her eyes quickly, not recognizing her surroundings. The events of the afternoon flooded her mind. Tears of relief stung her eyes.

"I should feel sorry for what happened to him, but I don't"

"I know."

"I am just so tired."

"Nurse this baby and go back to sleep. I will check on you both in a bit."

Mary left the young mother with the infant. Gracie attempted to stay awake while Hope nursed, but she drifted back into the blackness of exhaustion.

Mary folded her lightweight traveling coat into a make-shift pillow and covered herself with a small quilt she carried with her on her frequent trips. She was tired and the work of an evangelist was taxing to her middle-aged body. *This 'pillow' just as well be the rock that Jacob from the Bible used as a pillow.*

She put her tired feet up into the seat next to her and leaned against the window. It took a few minutes before she nodded off.

It is people like this poor little mother that keep me traveling from town to town and preaching in the little churches. There are a heap of folks in need.

She observed the people in the other seats in the passenger car. One couple in particular caught her eye. They seemed well matched. They spoke quietly and responded with frequent smiles.

She thought about her tragic marriage to the late Mr. Dewey. He had looked at her like she was livestock that would be used to build a herd. He asked how her health was and if she was strong. All he really cared about was her producing a male heir. She had done that. It was the only good thing that came from that marriage. Her son meant the world to her. She was very proud of the man Samuel Dewey turned into. He was a well-respected banker in Pueblo, Colorado. She was glad that he was not turned like his father. He had a tender heart. Even though his wife was not hospitable toward her and discouraged visits, Mary's frequent travels worried her son. He feared for her safety and health. He often asked her if she was lonely. He wanted to know if she would ever remarry.

Land sakes, it has been thirty years since I was married. What would I want a man bossing me around for? 'Sides, I don't know of a man who would allow his woman to preach.

While those thoughts mulled around in her head, she nodded off. The train sped down the track in the darkness of night.

*****

Mary brought Gracie her slat bonnet to cover her battered head.

"I figured you might want to go to the dining car and get something to eat. This will keep folks from gawking at you."

"Thank you," Gracie said as she tied the strings into a bow under her chin. "I look a sight with my cut-up scalp. I am sure it would trouble those with a weak stomach."

"You have been through a lot of distress, Gracie. I just want to save you from any more this morning."

"You have thought of everything! I will always remember your kindness."

They sat in the quiet dining car and ordered a large breakfast. Mary smiled at the young mother. "Do you want to tell me what happened and why he wanted to kill you?"

Gracie took a sip of coffee. Her large blue eyes clouded over and she adjusted Hope into the crook of her arm. "Phillip ran into hard luck with our ranch. He tried to raise some money by gambling and lost. We owed several men a lot of money. He heard that the Harmony Borax Works hired teams for $100 to $120 a month per team member. He told me I had to help with the mule team because, as a Swamper, I could make as much as he did as the Skinner. The plan was to pay back the money in ten months."

"How long have you been working the mule team?"

"We finished our third trip. Each trip took twenty days. We have been paid three times. Not one penny went to the debt. It looked like I would never get to go home and see my little boy again."

"You have a little boy?"

"He is only two. We have been gone over three months. I miss him so much! I asked the ticket clerk how much it cost to take the train on the last trip to Mojave."

"Where are you headed?"

"Trinidad, Colorado."

"Are you from there?"

"Mama and Daddy live there. They have my son."

Mary took a sip of the strong coffee and gave a slight nod. "We should pull into there by tomorrow evening."

"We can't get there soon enough."

"How did you break away from your husband?"

"The boss must have figured out that I am a woman because he dropped the gold coins that was my pay and knelt down and whispered for me to run as fast as I could. He and some other men started a fight with Phillip and held him back as long as possible. It was enough for me to get onto the train. I am so glad the porter kept him from reaching me."

"I don't know how you managed the heat on the trail to Mojave!"

"It was powerful hot. Little Hope felt like a hot water bottle tied to my body.

I couldn't believe the amount of sweat we produced. You wouldn't believe it, but it actually felt better wearing the long-sleeved shirt than going with only the chemise. The sun and wind burned my skin so quickly that I kept it on all the time. It was all that was protecting Hope. I was afraid that she would smother. Our sweat made the cloth wet and the harsh wind blew through it and cooled her off some. I spent as much time as possible in the small creeks at the overnight stops that had them. Hope was so hot that she didn't make a sound most of the time. I was afraid that she would die. I was afraid of being discovered. Every four days a new team started from the mine, so every four days we met a team on the way from Mojave. It was very difficult to hide Hope and not be discovered."

Gracie couldn't keep the tears from falling. Mary noted the sorrow on her face.

"Everything will turn out."

Gracie nodded and wiped her nose on the cloth napkin at her plate. "It has been so long since I left. I miss my son so much."

"Of course you do."

"He may not remember me."

"He will remember you."

Gracie leaned back in the chair. The bonnet hid the dark bruise on the side of her face, but her bruised spirit showed in her crystal blue eyes. Her shoulders sagged as she tended to the baby.

"Let me take care of her while you get some more sleep. You are still tired."

"I couldn't burden you with taking care of her like that."

"It has been years since my young'un was a baby. I enjoy caring for her. Let's get you back into that sleeping berth."

*****

Steam billowed from the engine as the train screeched to a stop at Trinidad, Colorado. Mary gave the girl a quick hug and tweaked the baby on the cheek.

"Take good care of this baby, Gracie."

"I will," she said as she stepped off the train.

Passengers disembarked as Mary sat watching the girl cross the platform and walk down the tree-lined street. "God, be with them."

Chapter 24

John fanned the fire with the old bellows. It burned hot and he plunged the horseshoe into the flame until the metal turned bright orange. He pulled it out onto the large anvil and began the toil of shaping it into use for the large work horse he was preparing it for.

The work was strenuous, but satisfying. He plunged the iron into the water reservoir and steam washed over his body. He looked at the product and nodded in contentment. The horse stood by and he ran his large hand down the muscular back and gave him a firm pat. The animal was powerful and even-tempered. He grabbed the hind leg and held it between his knees as he filed and shaped the hoof to receive the new shoe. He was well practiced in the work so the task was accomplished in good time.

Fred Young stood watching the smithy do the work. "Thank you for seeing to this so quick like. Nan wanted her garden plowed yesterday, but I couldn't put old Ned through the job with that old shoe draggin' like it was."

"No problem, Mr. Young. I am glad to do it."

"Looks like you have made a hand since you started up your blacksmith shop."

John Forrester wiped the sweat from his brow as he handed the reins to Fred.

"With a good word from you and your family, it made all the difference."

"Your work stands on its own merit."

"I appreciate that."

"You coming over for supper tonight? Nan and the girls have made fried chicken."

"I am afraid that I frequent your supper table too often, Fred."

"Nonsense. I don't think those women folk would ever have enough of your company."

"They must be powerfully lonesome if that is the truth," he said, laughing.

"You don't want to turn down Nan's fried chicken. I think Sally made a cherry pie today, also, and if I don't miss my guess, there will be plenty of mashed potatoes and more food than the law allows."

"You don't have to convince me. I have never had it so good."

"Why don't you head over as soon as you clean up? I want to have a chance to talk with you before the womenfolk take over," Fred said.

John went to the small room in the back of the building where he set up his bed and cook stove. He poured water into a basin and washed the day's grime off. He dried and pulled on a clean shirt. It smelled nice.

Since moving to Colorado, he had made a habit of taking his clothes to a lady who took in washing. She had a husband who frequented the saloon and refused to work.

It was up to her to keep body and soul together. John wanted to live a better life than he had in Boston, so he thought he would start with fresh, clean clothes. He didn't mind helping the good woman make a fair wage. *They aren't the finest quality clothes, but they make me feel like a new man.* Timothy had even told him that he walked with more confidence since he moved to Colorado.

I needed a new start. He quickly combed his damp hair and walked across the yard to Fred and Nan's house. Fred sat on the front porch.

"Sit with me a spell," Fred said.

"Don't mind if I do."

"I was just thinking about Timothy and how we came to know him."

"Yeah."

"Tim said that you sent him to Trinidad in the old trunk."

"I did."

"You know that the trunk belonged to Nan's mother and father?"

"No kiddin'? That is remarkable!"

"That *IS* remarkable," Fred stated.

John sat studying his hands. "There were some other things in that trunk."

"...other things?"

"...some clothes and a Bible..."

"Really, what happened to them?" Fred asked.

"I gave the clothes to the orphanage, but I kept the Bible."

Fred met John's gaze.

"It was because of what the woman, Nancy, wrote in that Bible that I found Jesus," John said.

"Isn't that something? Nancy was Nan's Ma."

"I still have it. I imagine that Nan will want it," John offered.

"Probably so. You can tell her."

The door creaked open. "Tell her what?" Nan asked.

"Hello, Mrs. Young. I was talking with Fred about the trunk I sent Tim to Colorado in."

"My mother's trunk?"

"I just now found out that it belonged to your mother. I did keep something ...the Bible...that was in it."

"Mama's Bible?"

"Your mother's Bible and her notes led me to the Lord," he said.

Tears slid down her smooth cheeks. "Oh, how very dear," she said.

"I will bring it to you after I copy down some of the notes of explanation she wrote in the pages...that is, if you don't mind."

"Of course I don't mind."

He stood and took her hand. "I am forever grateful for Nancy Johnson and her faith in God."

"I will replace the Bible with a new one. I wouldn't want you to go without having a good Bible," she said, squeezing his hand.

"You don't have to do that," he said.

"Ma would want me to. Now, if you are hungry, supper is ready."

Chapter 25

Gracie stepped onto the platform of the train station at Trinidad, clinging to her small baby. Tears swelled and burst in her eyes. She could barely see the steps leading onto the dusty street. The train had precious few passengers getting off or on, so there were only a couple of people around. She picked her way past the dozen houses between her childhood home and the station. No one saw her as she stood on the porch.

This was my home! Should I knock? What will Mama say? Will Papa allow me to stay? She brushed her knuckles against the door, knocking softly. Footsteps sounded on the board floor. She found herself face to face with her father as he carefully opened the door.

He placed his hands on each of her shoulders and drew her to his massive chest.

"Baby girl...my baby, what are you doing here? Come inside."

"Oh, Papa, I'm sorry. I had to come home."

"Phillip with you?" he asked.

"He...ah...died."

Emily Randall stepped inside the parlor and spotted her daughter. "Gracie! Are you all right? Is the baby all right? What name did you give to her? We never heard from you."

"Phillip named the baby 'Hope'. I felt that her name should have been 'Hopeless'."

"Where is Phillip?" she asked.

"He died," Gracie said flatly.

"Gracious!" Emily gasped.

"Where is Wayne? Is he all right?"

Emily nodded. "He is asleep for the night. He sleeps the whole night through now."

"Is he...does he miss me?"

"Oh, yes. He misses his mama," Clyde said.

Gracie took the slat bonnet off her head. Clyde whistled through his teeth.

"Girl, what in tarnation happened to you?"

"Death Valley...and...Phillip. I had to be disguised as a man. He shaved my head a couple of times with his hunting knife. Sometimes he sliced me. It mostly happened if he was drunk."

Emily took her into her arms and bumped into the sleeping baby.

"Little Hope, how did she fare? How did you hide her? Is she all right?"

"We are very tired, Mama."

"Of course you are. You look as if you have been to the brink and back," Emily said.

"I am afraid. We didn't get one penny sent to pay off Phillip's debts. I don't know what I am going to do."

"Why don't you bed down next to Wayne? We will iron out this mess in the morning. You look dead on your feet."

"Thanks, Papa."

"Go on to bed now, girl. You can tell us all about it tomorrow."

Gracie put Hope in the old cradle next to the small bed in the room. *Thank the Lord Papa never moved anything out of the house once it came in.* Emily stepped inside the room and pressed a finger to her lips while pressing a clean nightgown into her hands. Gracie hugged her mother and quickly donned the gown and slipped under the covers next to Wayne. The child snuggled close and put his pudgy arms around her neck. She breathed in the scent of him. Tears dripped from her eyes. *I am home, baby boy, I will never leave you again!* Her muscles relaxed as she heard his steady breathing. Her sleep was deep and sweet.

*****

Bright sunlight streamed through the lace curtains. Gracie sat up quickly and looked around the familiar room. Wayne and Hope slept. She quietly dressed and sat in the old rocker next to the wide window. She looked out without seeing the trees and neighbor's home. She heard Phillip's screams and saw blood pouring where his legs were severed from his body. *Is he dead? Surely he died. Oh God, I hope he is dead!* She looked down at her trembling hands. *God, is it wrong for me to hope he is dead?* She shook her head as if to shake the thoughts from her brain. Standing, she smoothed the front of the old dress and stepped out of the room to find her mother in the kitchen.

"You are up earlier than I thought, Gracie. Are you sure you rested enough?" Emily asked.

"I am fine, Mama."

Emily poured coffee into a delicate china cup and handed it to her. "Watch out, it is hot. It boiled over just before you came in."

Gracie took the cup and sprinkled a spoon of sugar into it. She poured a bit of coffee from the cup into the saucer, blew on it, and carefully sipped. "Hmm very good. I don't know how you do it, but nobody beats your coffee."

Emily smiled at her daughter. "It is good to have you home again."

Gracie finished the sips from the saucer and placed her cup back on it. "I have missed you and Papa so much."

"We never should have let you go to California with Phillip."

"You didn't have a choice. He was my husband."

"Yes."

Gracie shifted in her chair. "He died in an accident."

"On the mule team?"

"No."

"How?"

"He...it is a long story."

"We have time, sweetie. Just tell Mama what happened."

Gracie rubbed her sweaty hands on the front of her dress. "He drank a lot. He gambled what he didn't spend on whiskey every time we were paid. I managed to pilfer some away to buy a train ticket home, but didn't have enough."

"Oh."

"The boss man figured out that I was a woman and helped me get away. I was able to keep the money I was paid for my wage." She stood and walked to the stove to refill her cup. "The boss and some other fellows beat him up. While they fought with him, I ran with Hope to the train station. He came after me."

"Dear me!"

"He screamed out my name and jumped onto the train. If I had gotten on the last passenger car, he would have been able to stop me. When he lunged toward the next car, he slipped and fell onto the tracks. The wheels cut his legs off."

Emily gasped and put her hands over her mouth.

"Someone pulled him off the tracks. They didn't help him. They went through his pockets and stole his money. I think he died there...I hope he died there."

Emily put her arms around her daughter. "Me, too."

"I hated him, Mama! I never hated anyone so much!" she fairly screamed, then quietly added, "I think he hated me, too."

Emily held her close and gently patted her back. "My girl doesn't hate easily. He was a horrible man to put you through...everything."

"I don't like hating."

"I know."

Gracie pulled back and looked into her mother's eyes. Emily noted the fear in the blue orbs. "I am still afraid of him. I wish I knew that he was dead."

"We will talk to Papa when he gets home. He will know what to do," Emily said.

Gracie nodded. "I think I hear Wayne stirring," she said as she hastily went to the bedroom. "Mama's here, sweetheart. Mama is never going to leave you again."

Wayne smiled, revealing new teeth acquired during her absence. "Mama!" His chubby arms held her in a vise grip. She threw a look to the cradle and noticed that Hope's eyes were open. She took Wayne to the cradle and said, "This is your baby sister, Hope. Do you remember when she was born?"

Hope heard her name called and smiled. Kicking her legs, she squealed when Wayne reached in and touched her hand. *Poor little thing is afraid to make much noise. Maybe she can be a normal baby now.* Gracie picked her up and kissed her on the cheek. "You both are my precious angels."

"Where is Poppy?" Wayne asked.

"He has gone to hel...heaven," she stammered.

Chapter 26

Timothy Forrester sniffed the fresh smell of sage on the range of Ted Young's ranch. He sat proud in the saddle of his newly acquired horse. It was a large buckskin gelding named Butterscotch. He slid out of the saddle and knelt next to the pond where Butterscotch drank. The water was clear and he was hot, so he doffed his clothes and dove in. The swim was refreshing in the heat of the day. He felt strong and healthy. Living at the ranch provided him with good nourishing food and hard work. His mind felt strong as well. He found working with Ted and Manda a joy. Ralph and Edna adopted him as their would-be grandson. They always found something for him that they knew he needed. Butterscotch was one of those 'things'.

He floated on his back and looked at the well-muscled horse. His mind traveled back to Chowder. That horse would always be the horse of his dreams. He figured he would never see her again. After the gang made him sell Chowder, it nearly broke his heart. *The Old Man really knew how to break your spirit.*

He thought about his time as a captive.

Victoria was a broken person, too. I am just glad I got away. He flipped over and swam quickly across the pond and back. *Was Henry an angel? How did he hide me from the gang?* He shook his head and made his way to the bank of the pond. Butterscotch nickered a greeting. "Well, boy, I don't know much, but I do know that you are a trophy. I owe Ralph and Edna a lot for giving you to me."

He dressed and climbed on Butterscotch's back. He had finished checking fence and all was well on the Young ranch. *I will stop in and tell Ted that I would like to go see Uncle John.*

*****

"How in the world are you, Tim?"

Timothy pulled back from his uncle's warm embrace. "I feel human again."

"You look good. Ya want something to eat?"

"Sure."

John couldn't help laughing at the boy. Timothy's grin spread the entire width of his face. He studied Timothy closely. "I can't say as I have ever seen you this happy."

"It's the buckskin. Ralph gave him to me. He is a pleasure to ride."

"How long have you had him?"

"Nigh unto a week. We have been fixin' fence and checkin' cattle so I haven't had an opportune time to come into town to show 'im to ya. You gettin' on all right here?"

"I can't say as I have ever been more at home in my life. Here, I made a big mess of stew and only had a bowl of it for dinner. There is plenty for our supper," John said.

The two sat at the small table and savored the tasty meal. Each was lost in thoughts of the past.

"This is a world away from Boston," Timothy said.

"My thoughts exactly," John answered as he tipped his chair on the back legs and leaned against the wall. "You know, it wasn't you that your pa was against."

"What do you mean?"

"It was the cruel world we grew up in. Many wrong things happened to the both of us. He dealt with his hurts in a bottle and I... I tried to work myself to death. I am glad he made peace with God before he died. It is good that he saw you and was able to set things straight with you, too."

"It meant a lot to me," Timothy said.

They sat in comfortable stillness for the remainder of the simple meal.

"Good cornbread, Uncle."

"Thanks."

Timothy scooted back his chair and took the tin plate to the wash pan. He washed it slowly and placed it upside down on the sideboard. "You know what? The Bible says that it is a man's place to wash dishes. That's what Edna says."

"Do tell?"

"In II Kings 22:13 it says that God will wipe out Jerusalem as a man wipeth a dish, wiping it, and turning it upside down."

"I can imagine that Edna found that Scripture to be quite handy," John said, chuckling.

"You should have heard Ralph howl over that one. She had to get her Bible out and show it to him before he believed her."

"Here I was thinking on finding a wife so that I could get her to wash my dishes."

Timothy's smile broadened. "Do you have anyone in mind? Are you thinking on June or Sally?"

"Heaven help me, no! Those girls are closer to your age than mine. Why aren't you sparkin' them? They are really pretty girls."

Timothy's face turned bright red. "I ...ah...don't know."

"It would appear that we are both leaning on the side of shy. At this rate, neither one us will ever wed whether we want to wash dishes forever or not."

"Uncle, did you ever try to leave Boston before?"

John locked his fingers behind his head. He stared at the far corner of the small room before he answered, "I couldn't leave Cecil. I think I needed him as much and he needed me."

"I am glad you were always there...for me, too. The food you snuck to me kept me alive."

"You were a bright spot in my life, Tim."

"So, tell me about your ideal woman."

John chuckled and sat all four chair legs on the floor. He leaned forward and placed his arms on the table. "Probably any woman who would be dumb enough to tolerate me. You?"

"I was sweet on a girl who helped me learn how to read when I first got here and went to school. She is married and has a couple of babies now."

"Tough luck, pard. As young as you are, you will have other chances."

Timothy punched his uncle playfully on the arm and stood. "I best head back to the ranch. Sun up comes pretty quick if you haven't slept much."

John followed him out the front door of the livery stable and watched him ride away.

*****

Timothy turned Butterscotch down the old familiar path to Gracie's house. Talking about her with John stirred up thoughts of the old feelings. It wasn't much out of the way so he wouldn't be wasting much time. He rode down the quiet street and noted the light in the windows of several houses. Gracie's house still had a light lit in the parlor. He saw that someone sat on the old rocker on the porch. He stopped the horse and eased out of the saddle. As he strode up the path to the house, he waved at Mr. Randall. "How are you, Mr. Randall?"

"Hello, Timothy. Things are looking up."

"How so?"

"Gracie is home. She is finally home."

Timothy's mouth went dry. "Phillip decided to come on back?"

"She came back alone with baby Hope."

Timothy frowned and pondered the statement.

Clyde stood and stepped off the porch to speak face to face with Timothy, "Phillip is dead. She came home to heal."

"Sorry...I am sorry for her loss."

"She has been through a lot and looks like something the cat drug in. You will need to give her time before you come to see her."

"Is she all right? Is she sick?"

"She is very frail. The work in Death Valley almost did her in. Her skin is burned and that maniac almost butchered her when he shaved her head."

"Shaved her head?" Timothy clenched his fists at his side. "I don't care what she looks like. I need to see for myself that she is all right. Please ask her if I can talk to her."

"Come sit in the rocker and I will go to her. I won't make her talk to you."

Timothy nodded.

Clyde disappeared into the house and Timothy waited for several minutes before the door opened. He blinked back tears when he saw her. She had a large bandana tied tightly to her scalp. The dress she wore hung on her emaciated frame. She smiled carefully at him and he noted her sunken cheeks. He stood quickly and gathered her in his arms carefully.

"Gracie, you don't know how much I have missed you!" he said with tears stuck in his throat.

Gracie stepped out of his embrace and looked into his face. "You have grown up!"

"Is that a bad thing?" he asked, laughing.

"No. You turned out really...nice..." she said quietly.

"You did, too." He drew her close to his heart. He whispered close to her ear, "I have missed you. When I needed something good to think about, I thought about you."

She allowed him to hold her close. The feel of his strong arms poured strength into her very spirit. Tears ran down her cheeks and she sniffed loudly. He pulled her back at arm's length and looked into her stormy eyes.

"I never wanted to leave. It is a long story."

"Please tell me. I want to know."

He took a deep breath and took her to the rocker. He sat in the chair beside it and placed his elbows on his knees. "I ran away from my father in Boston because he hated me. He told me he was going to kill me."

"Dear me!"

"I thought I had started a new life here. When I left your house the night I brought Chowder here to show her to you, I saw Uncle John and him getting off the train. I had to get away."

"I see."

"I ran poor Chowder nearly to death. I stopped to stay in a stable to give her some rest.

Some outlaws forced me to go with them to their hide-out. I was held captive for years before I got away. I have been back nearly three months."

"I left three months ago."

"Phillip is dead?"

"I think so."

He noted the tired lines around her mouth. *It must be a long story.* "I am sorry for your loss. You look tired. I will be back to see you if that is all right with you."

"That would be nice."

He stood and helped her to her feet. The beautiful blue eyes were clouded with fatigue. "Get some rest, Gracie. I will be back."

He left her standing on the porch and mounted the horse. She seemed to be a shell of the girl he had known. "Goodbye, Gracie," he said as he turned the horse to go.

She watched him disappear into the night. "Goodbye."

Gracie watched Timothy until he was out of sight. She quietly went into her room and slipped into the old bed next to her children. She was too tired to undress. The soft, even breathing of her babies sounded peaceful. She listened and marveled at the solace they brought in their total innocence. Her tired mind no longer saw Phillip bleeding on the tracks and handled roughly by strangers.

She reflected on the kind face of her childhood friend. *Timothy, it was so good to see you.*

Soon her slow, even breathing joined that of her children.

Emily opened the door and noted that Gracie was still dressed. She carefully removed the lace-up shoes and covered the precious daughter with an old quilt from the foot of the bed. She kissed her sunken cheek.

"God, thank you for bringing my girl back to me. Please give her strength."

She soundlessly left the room and closed the door. Gracie dreamed of the comforting, strong arms.

*****

Timothy took the few miles to the ranch slowly. He gave Butterscotch his head. He sensed the mood of his master and adjusted his temperament to him. The sky was clear and the stars were large. *Goodness sakes, they look like big old eggs ready to be gathered and put into a basket!* The night air was crisp. It was a far cry from the heat of the afternoon. Some of the stars twinkled. He wondered at the vastness of the sky-canvas stretched out before him.

His mood was thoughtful. *How can I be both happy and sad to see Gracie? Phillip is dead. Is that what she said? Somehow, she wasn't sure? Why did she marry him? He was always a brute in school. She looked bad...half-dead... what did that miserable man do to her?*

He arrived at the ranch and bedded Butterscotch down.

He didn't want to talk with anyone, so he went straight to his bunk. He prepared for bed and slipped under the rough wool covers. Before he nodded off, he saw sad, crystal blue eyes. *I want to see them sparkle again.*

Chapter 27

John sat in the small pie shop sipping strong, hot coffee and plunging his fork into a piece of apple pie. He took a large bite and savored the flavor of brown sugar, cinnamon, and firm apples. He looked through the lace curtains onto the street. It was mid-day, and, even though it was not his custom to close shop at the noon hour, he broke with routine and searched out his favorite pie. *Sometimes a man's gotta enjoy something unnecessary.* He didn't attempt to keep the smile from his lips.

The waitress refilled his cup and noted the smile. "Mr. Forrester, I see that you are enjoying the pie."

"Absolutely."

"Let me know if you need anything else."

His eyes followed her as she disappeared through the door to the kitchen. He was one of five customers in the establishment. He took inventory of them and noted that he had met all of them. The townspeople were friendly and in need of another smithy. *I am glad I moved here.*

A tall, thin man stopped at his table. "Good to see you again, John. I hope you can come to the evening meeting at the little stone church tonight."

"Sure, Stretch, save me a seat," John said.

Stretch donned his hat and walked through the door.

John watched him cross the street and enter the dry goods store. *At least a church meeting is something different to do.* He finished the pie and coffee and resumed his work for the day.

*****

The little stone church had a good number of people in it. It was more than half full when John found Stretch in the second pew from the back on the right side of the narrow aisle. There was a lot of chatter amongst the congregants. John heard the words 'woman preacher'. He detected that the words were not said in a charitable fashion. More likely they were attached to a snarl.

Reverend Morgan called the meeting to order in his usual quiet fashion. "Brothers and Sisters, we are blessed to have Sister Mary Dewey with us this evening to speak. She wanted me to point out from the beginning that she is not going to preach to you, but she wants to give glory to God for the changes He made in her life. She wants to be an encouragement to this body of believers, as well as to those who have not put their trust in God. Sister Dewey, will you tell us the things that are on your heart tonight?"

Mary Dewey quietly stood next to the pulpit and shook Reverend Morgan's hand. 'Quiet' was the best description John could think of when he saw her. She was middle-aged and small

. She couldn't have been over five foot tall. Her blond hair was lightened with a few gray streaks and pulled back into a bun.

Small ringlets escaped the combing back and framed her face. She had large, intelligent brown eyes that leveled a sincere gaze at each person in the small crowd.

"I do want you to know that I don't claim to be a preacher. I do claim to be a changed person. Because of the changes that Jesus has made in my life, I feel driven to tell others that there is hope for them.

"I started out all right in my life. I was from a large family and we all got along just fine. My heart was broken by the boy I was engaged to, so I married the first man who asked. I was getting to the stage where folks were starting to say the words 'old maid' and 'unclaimed blessing'. "

The congregation chuckled quietly as she continued. "You might say that I became bitter after I married Mr. Dewey. He took a strap to me many times to keep me under control. He had some step-children from his wife who had passed away weeks before he met me. In fact, some of you know my step-children. They are Dr. Elmer Johnson and Mrs. Fred Young."

John noticed several women whispering to their spouses. He leaned forward in rapt attention.

"Nan and Elmer were very young. I was only eight years older than Nan. I wanted them to respect me.

I wanted to control them. I wanted them to need me, but they had each other. I was very jealous of the love they had for each other. I was cruel to them. I beat Nan many times. She never did one thing to deserve the beatings." Mary hung her head as tears dripped down her face.

"I didn't know what I was doing. I had a man who hated me, but wanted to produce an heir so that he could get his family's inheritance. My family had taught me that I could never come back home if I got into a fix. I took out my hurt on those kids."

She took her hankie and dabbed her swollen red eyes. "They ran away to safety. I have to say that I am so glad they did. I didn't even look for them because I had become such a monster that I didn't recognize myself. I wanted them to get away from me and Mr. Dewey."

"After they left, I decided to make myself into a better person. It was like doing schoolwork and spilling ink on the page. I needed a new page. I thought I could do it myself. I figured that I would dress better, make affluent friends, go to the biggest church, and join as many committees that I could fit in. That would make me the kind of woman people would respect.

"I soon found out that I was still the same unhappy person I had always been. The only difference was that I was tired and the committee chairwomen took advantage of my willingness to work and be accepted.

"My husband did treat me better because I took care with my appearance and tried to talk in a more kind way to him. I was with child so he quit beating me. He left to take care of his dying mother and I went to a special meeting at the church. The speaker presented Jesus as I had never heard of Him. He read the passage in the Bible where Jesus said that He came to bind up the broken-hearted and to preach deliverance to the captive. He asked those who wanted to be free from religion, sin, and heartbreak to come to the front and pray.

"I looked around the room and there were all these people that I had fooled into thinking that I was a good lady. I wondered what they would think if I went up front and prayed with the man. My soul was hurting so bad that I didn't care. I went up there and prayed like I had never prayed before. The preacher's wife prayed with me and so did the speaker. After I laid out all the pain I had been in and had caused, I felt this lightness inside that is hard to explain. There were no dark corners inside of me. I didn't have to pretend to be good.

"The Bible says that Jesus puts His robe of righteousness around us. Our righteousness is like filthy rags. I laid down those self-righteous rags and let Him put His robe on me. I became a new creature in Jesus Christ.

"Even though my heart was right with God, I needed to figure out how to find Nan and Elmer and apologize. I needed to tell them that they didn't have to be afraid of me anymore.

I came to Trinidad because the speaker was from here. I went to his house to ask him how to go about making things right with those kids. When I got to the door, Nan opened it! She was the wife of the speaker.

"God worked everything out. He gave Nan and Elmer the strength to forgive me. After Mr. Dewey died, I knew that I had to go to churches and tell my story. I must tell everyone how wonderful Jesus is and how He can take a broken life and make it over. He made me brand new and He will do the same for you."

Reverend Morgan took the pulpit and stretched out his large hands. "If there are any here who need to pray and put things to rights with God, please come to the altar."

John noticed several standing and finding a place to kneel. Although he had already made peace with God, he felt compelled to pray at the altar for the ability to let his past go. He liked hearing Sister Dewey speak about Jesus' healing the broken hearted. *I am a broken man. I need God to put me back together again.* "God, take these shattered pieces of my life and make something good out of them. Thank You for forgiving my sins and being my Savior. I just need to feel whole inside."

The service came to a close and John found Mary at the door of the church. She extended her hand and he took it, giving her a firm but gentle shake. "Sister Dewey, I appreciate your message. It helped me take care of some things in my past."

"Good."

He held her hand a little long and shyly pulled away. "Would you care to walk a bit?"

Mary glanced at Reverend Morgan. He said, "Mildred and I will see you at the parsonage."

Chapter 28

A full moon lit the road to the parsonage. John nervously cleared his throat. "Mrs. Dewey, I have some questions about your ...ah...speech tonight," he said as he gathered his courage to continue, "The things you talked about are unbelievable."

Mary turned and looked directly at him. He quickly bowed his head and looked at his feet, avoiding eye contact.

She blinked hard, saying, "It is true."

"I believe you. It is just very hard to believe that you would tell all of this to strangers, especially since you are a preacher."

"Sometimes I tell people that I am a preacher because it is easier to say than to explain what I do. I have been given the gift of forgiveness and I have to tell people about it."

He frowned and began walking slowly. She fell into step with him. "I have to tell people how Jesus can change the worst person into...someone with purpose."

"The only priest I ever knew didn't care about anyone."

She stopped in front of the parsonage. "Tell me," she said.

"He hated all of us."

"Who?"

"The kids in the orphanage... he tortured us. He killed my little brother," he said. John sat on the top step of the parsonage porch.

"...sorry."

"How can someone who is 'devoted to God' do things like that?" he asked.

"I don't know. Tell me what happened."

He covered his face with his hands and pulled them through his hair. "I can't tell that. I do have a question, though. I never knew a preacher that I could ask."

"All right."

"Clarence's death was vicious. He was a little guy and I always thought that he was out there somewhere wishing that he could have lived a long life. I felt that he blamed Cecil and me for not stopping the priest."

"Oh?"

"Not long ago, I had a dream about him. It was so real. I thought I was actually with him. He told me that the pain didn't last long for him. Almost immediately, he was in a beautiful place. He told me he was very happy. He wanted me to be happy. Could this be true?"

"I only know what I have read in the Bible. There is a passage where Jesus talks about a poor man named Lazarus who died and was taken to Abraham's bosom. I think it was known as 'Paradise'.

If you read in the book of Revelation, there are wonderful descriptions of heaven.

It sounds to me like your dream was that Clarence went to heaven."

"Why would I have a dream like that?" he asked.

"I would guess that God wanted to comfort you. I don't know you, but it seems that you have been stuck in the past. You have not escaped your childhood."

"You are much like me. You seem to have to tell how bad you were and not go on with your life."

Mary's eyes widened and filled with tears. She turned away from him and said, "I am doing the Lord's work."

John stood and put his hand on her elbow, turning her around to face him. "Do you have anything else besides your speaking?" he asked.

"I have a son who lives in Pueblo, Colorado. He is married and is very busy working as a banker."

"You do have more in your life than speaking, then."

"Not really. His wife told me that Samuel is ashamed of me because I have told my story all over the place. He wants to advance into politics and being connected with me would hold him back. She asked that I break my relationship with him to help him out."

"So you have lost your son because of this...speaking?" he asked.

She sighed and closed her mouth in a thin line.

"I must apologize. I don't even know you," he said.

"You are right. I have lost my son."

"I know Elmer and Nan. Why weren't they at the meeting tonight?" he asked.

She frowned and answered, "They have moved on. Is that what you want to hear?"

"Aren't you and Nan friends now? You are both Christians."

"The story is a painful one and I don't ask them to come and relive those experiences. They are kind to me. It is because of their forgiveness that I know that the forgiveness of God is real."

"It doesn't appear that you have prospered in this line of work. Why do you do it?"

"I tell my story to help people know that God can do anything with anyone."

"Mary Dewey, you are an amazing woman."

She topped the steps and turned to give him a smile before she put her hand on the doorknob.

"I want to see you again," he said.

She said, "Thank you for the talk."

John watched her pass through the door.

Chapter 29

Mary slipped through the door and greeted Reverend Morgan and his wife, Mildred. She gave a shy smile to her hosts.

"It was a beautiful night for a walk, Mrs. Dewey," said Mildred.

"Yes, it was nice."

"John is from back East. I think I heard 'Boston'. Isn't that right, Brother Morgan?" Mildred asked.

"Yes, he is. He is also a very good smithy."

"Of course, *you would* think like a man. I am thinking that he is different than regular folk around here. Why, it is almost as if he were a foreigner. I would think that you would do well to watch your association with him," the pastor's wife said.

Mary removed her simple bonnet and smoothed her hair as she turned to address Mildred's comment. "Sister Morgan, I have traveled to Boston and met with many good Christian people. I have also been to California and found believers there as well. People are just people," she said.

Mildred drew in her breath and screeched, "Well!" She narrowed her eyes and continued,

"Mrs. Dewey, I am thinking that you consider yourself an expert on godliness. You may 'say' that you don't call yourself a 'preacher' and that you are just telling your story, but I think that this has gone to your head. I refuse to be instructed by a woman preacher."

Mary squared her shoulders and glanced at the reverend and back to his wife before she said, "You may speak ill of me, but please do not allow yourself to belittle other believers. I have testified of God's forgiveness and grace toward me. I have tried to point to Him as the One and only One who can change someone as vile as me into a grateful child of God. I am not an expert in anything, except the experience I have had regarding God's mercy. I have not meant to do anything to hurt you."

Mildred pursed her lips and put her hands on her hips. "Brother Morgan! Brother Morgan, are you going to allow this?" she asked.

"Mildred, go on to bed and shut your mouth," he said. "Sister Dewey, it is probably best that you retire for the night. I appreciate the burden on your heart to minister to people, but there are others who do not understand. We will be cancelling the rest of the meetings for the week. I will compensate you for your travel expense and a small amount for your efforts with our congregation."

Mary ducked her head and whispered, "Thank you, Reverend Morgan."

She stepped quietly through the doorway to the small bedroom she was assigned to.

Every item in the room was old and worn. The bed was rusty and the chair had cotton spilling out of the large arms. She sat on the edge of the bed. It had an old feather tick on it. *This is better than most places I sleep in my travels.*

She stood and quickly undressed and put on her long nightgown. She stood in front of the cracked mirror and pulled the long hairpins from the large bun at the nape of her neck. Wispy curls framed her face. They had escaped the confines of the bun long before her speech. The curls did help give her plain face some character. She pulled the long blond hair over her shoulder and began to brush out the tangles. She made short work of it because she was tired to the bone.

She stretched out on the old bed. The tiredness of her body ignored the lumpiness of the tick. Her mind raced. First, Mr. Forrester had questioned her motives in speaking. Then, Mrs. Morgan spoke her mind. *Maybe I need to just stay home and stop all of this.* She felt a cold chill. *I don't have a home! Sammy sold the farm that Nan deeded to me.* She pulled the covers up to her chin. *I will just stay at the rooming house in Denver. I at least have friends there.* She started to drift off to sleep and awoke with a start. *How will I support myself? I have preached for twenty-nine years! I am fifty-two years old. What kind of work can I do?*

Thoughts swirled in her mind until the wee hours of the night.

Finally, she whispered, "Lord God, I am willing to do whatever You want me to do. I will also stop if that is what You want. Please, make the pathway clear to me."

*****

Mary awoke early and walked to the train station to take the early train to Denver. John saw her with her valise in her hand waiting on the platform. He sprinted across the street to where she stood.

"Mrs. Dewey, I thought you were going to be in Trinidad throughout the week."

"That was the plan, but...ah...plans changed," she said.

He searched her face and didn't discover any clues, so he asked, "What kind of plans would that be?"

She looked into his face with guileless eyes and cleared her throat, saying, "Plans to not have a 'woman preacher' speak at this particular church in Trinidad." She noted the angry look on his face and added, "It is really all right. I am used to it. I am in prayer as to whether this will continue to be my vocation."

"Where are you going?" he asked.

"I live in Denver when I am not speaking."

"I want to see you again. Could I see you someday?"

She took out her embroidered handkerchief and dabbed the tears from her eyes and blew her nose softly. "You don't have to worry about me, Mr. Forrester."

"It isn't that. I admire your courage. I...haven't known many women before...and...you are...I don't know. It seems that you are real."

"Real?"

He paced in front of her and stopped as he heard the train whistle announcing its approach to town. "I...ah...It seems that most women need flowery talk and such. I don't know how to be anyone else but myself. Is that good enough for you?" he asked.

She shook her head and dabbed her eyes.

The train pulled into the station and steam drifted up to them as they stood on the platform. "Where can I find you in Denver, Mrs. Dewey?" he asked.

"Mrs. Langley's Boarding House...located three blocks north of the library."

"Will you see me...ah...go to dinner with me if I look you up?"

She smiled her answer.

"Is that a yes?"

"Yes!" she exclaimed as she stepped onto the train. She found her seat and saw him on the platform. He searched the windows of the passenger cars. She placed her hand on the window and he saw the movement. He saw her and came close to the window.

"See you soon," he said.

She hadn't noticed how bright his smile was until that moment. He looked like she had imagined the angel Gabriel would look. He stood tall and strong. *He reminds me of Lester, my first love.* She sighed. *Only Lester didn't really love me as much as I loved him, else he wouldn't have run away with my cousin on the eve of our wedding.*

The train moved slowly from the station and soon he was out of view. *Time does heal. I don't even cry when I think of Lester anymore.*

Chapter 30

John Forrester watched as Mary Dewey disappeared into the distance. He started across the street to the restaurant and noticed that Dr. Johnson entered the establishment only a few steps before he did. He scanned the room and saw that Elmer was sitting at a corner table.

"Dr. Johnson, may I join you?"

"Only if you call me 'Elmer' or 'Doc'."

"Thank you, Elmer. I would like to talk with you about someone I have just met."

The waitress gave the men steaming hot coffee. Elmer ventured a sip. "Oh?"

"Mary Dewey, I met Mary Dewey. What do you think of her?"

"You do know that she used to be my Ma?"

"Stepmother, right?"

"Yes, so I don't know if I am objective about her."

"So you haven't forgiven her for being so mean to you and Nan?"

Elmer took a large gulp of the hot coffee. He felt it all the way down his throat to his stomach. He tented his fingers on the table in front of the coffee cup. Leveling his gaze at John, he said, "I was only five years old. I remember being afraid, especially for Nan, but Mary is not the same woman she was then. If ever a person changed, it has been Mary Dewey."

"My brother changed like that. I guess that is one reason she interests me. Cecil never was...kind, but after he became a Christian, he wanted to make up for being evil."

"Cecil did seem to carry a lot of guilt. I only knew him after he was Saved," Elmer said.

"I am drawn to Mary Dewey. I feel protective toward her, like I want to take care of her."

Elmer scooted his chair back and put both hands flat on the table saying, "You are sweet on Mrs. Dewey?"

John put the coffee cup to his mouth and nodded his head. The waitress came with their order of pancakes and bacon with butter and maple syrup.

"Do you gents need anything else?" she asked.

Elmer laughed loudly, asking, "Do you have anything for a lovesick old pup?"

"Now, you could have gone all day without saying that!" John said as he realized that he possibly had fallen in love. *Over fifty and getting lovesick, me?*

"So, Elmer, how old are you? I would guess over thirty. Am I right? Are you lovesick yet?"

The smile vanished from his face as quickly as it had appeared. "No. I will probably be a bachelor until I die."

"Not you! Never. I have seen the women when they are around you."

Elmer studied the man's face. This man was someone who didn't feel that he already knew him like all the people in Trinidad did.

From the few times he and John had spoken, he felt that he could be trusted. He began, "There is someone, but she would not leave her work."

"Not even to be with you?"

"When I was at medical school in Denver, I was assigned to care for the children at the orphanage. One of the caretakers was a beautiful young woman named Constance Brooks. She is dedicated to her job, because she protects the little ones from abuse."

John saw the sad look in Elmer's eyes as he spoke. "So, she won't marry you?"

"She doesn't know me. I guess you could say that I love her from afar."

"Now, aren't we a sorry mess! How in the world did we let this happen to us?" John asked.

Elmer grinned and dove into the last few bites of his pancakes. "I am thinking that you would make Mary Dewey a fine husband."

"Me, too."

Chapter 31

Mary was not conscious of the tears that streaked her face. The scenery that passed before the glass was only a blur. Her stomach had done several flip-flops in the minutes after John had disappeared from view. She felt as if she had been kicked in the gut. Many times she rode the train back to Denver, days earlier than she was originally scheduled to. The reason people couldn't understand why she felt compelled to tell her story, she would never know.

Her mind twisted into knots about John. *Why did John want to meet me? Why did he care? Does he care? He seems authentic.* She shifted in her seat and dabbed her eyes with her hanky. *He asked about my financial situation, so he knows that I am poverty-stricken. That rules out someone who would think he could get financial gain.* The thought brought a smirk to her lips. *Me, wealthy? Now that would be bizarre.*

She put her hand to her cheek. *I am not pretty or interesting. Why would he want to come to Denver to have dinner with me?* She saw her reflection in the window. Tired lines formed around her mouth. She leaned her head against the seat and slept fitfully for a few moments.

In those minutes she was seventeen years old again. The summer breeze caught one of the blond curls that rested on her shoulder. Lester pressed his lips to hers.

Her heart hammered in her ears. He pulled her to his chest and laughed. "Girl, I can feel your heartbeat!"

She tilted her head back and allowed his mouth to devour hers. She pulled back from his hungry mouth and whispered, "Wait, Lester, we will be married tomorrow. I will be yours tomorrow."

She heard a sound in the bushes beside them. Her cousin, Bessie, held her hand over her mouth and allowed a loud giggle to escape.

"Who do we have here?" Lester asked.

Mary scowled and remarked through gritted teeth, "It is only my cousin, Bessie. Bessie, what are you doing here?"

Lester turned toward the girl and commanded, "Let's have a look at you. Show yourself."

Bessie stepped from behind the bush and flashed a bright smile. Her cheeks were vivid from embarrassment. Mary stood dumbstruck at the beauty of the girl. Her lips were deep pink to match her cheeks. Long dark lashes matched the tumbled-down curls that reached her tiny waist. Mary heard the quick intake of breath as Lester assessed the young woman.

"What are you doing here?" he asked.

She sauntered up to him and put her hand on his arm. In a mere whisper she said, "I was afraid I wouldn't have a chance to kiss the groom tomorrow."

Mary turned her head quickly and saw his eyes.

The play of fire in them was unmistakable. She knew, then, that she had lost him.

The train bumped along the track and Mary awoke. The same old scene played in her mind. Her face burned crimson once again as she recalled the words of her mother the morning that was to have been her wedding day, "Lester's done run off with your cousin Bessie. Hold your head up high, girl. We will do what we can to keep you from being an old maid."

How could actions and words from so long ago still be so painful? She smoothed the front of her dress and sat straighter in her seat. *I won't ever trust another man again.*

She thought of John. He had seemed honest with her. He had even asked her hard questions about her life. His honesty was almost unbearable. She felt that he could determine immediately if she were telling the truth. *Maybe I will trust John, but I won't love him. I will not love again.*

Chapter 32

Timothy found himself knocking on Gracie's screen door for the third evening in a row. Wayne opened the door and grabbed him around the legs in a tight hug. Timothy pretended to struggle, then lifted the boy over his head and tossed him up a few inches and caught him. The child squealed with laughter. Gracie watched the exchange with a contented sigh.

"Gracie, I need to talk with you about something important."

"All right, Timothy."

"Are you going to stand on ceremony and go through the year-long grieving process over Phillip?"

Gracie's face turned as white as a marble sculpture. "Grieve...I...ah... am not sure he is dead!" she said, covering her face and sobbing.

Timothy put a clumsy arm around her shoulders. "I am a dope. I don't know what to say. I guess I was wondering how long we would have to wait to get married."

"Married?"

"I'm sorry. You are grieving. I better go." He jumped up and ran out the screen door before Gracie could gather her thoughts.

She sat down hard in a kitchen chair and stared. *Grief? Death? Is Phillip really dead?*

Clyde saw his daughter's stricken look when he entered the kitchen with an armload of firewood. He sat at the table and took her hand. "What is it, baby girl?" he asked.

"Phillip... I need to know if Phillip is still alive."

He rubbed the stubble on his chin while he thought over her predicament. Then he placed his big, rough hand on hers. "Mojave? Is that where it happened?" he asked.

"Yes."

"I can't stand to see what this uncertainty has done to you. I will go on the first train and see what I can find out." He pulled her into his arms. "Papa will see to it. No need for you to pine away."

"Papa...I...hope he is dead."

"I know. We will both know the truth soon."

Chapter 33

Clyde Randall felt the burning of bile as it rose into his throat. The smell of ripe flesh was more than his sensibilities could stand, so he stepped outside the run-down shack to rid himself of his breakfast. He stepped back into the offending room and stared at the man who was his son-in-law.

Phillip was broken. He had lost both legs to the wheels of the east bound train. He lay with a smirk on his face despite the high fever that raged in his body. Clyde detested the sorry excuse of a man, but he knew his duty as the father-in-law. "Doc, when can he travel?"

The doctor's eyes were lost behind the bushy eyebrows as they pushed together in a deep furrow. He shook his head and muttered, "This one be mostly dead. The only way he would live through the trip you are talkin' about would be out of sheer meanness."

"I will live, old man!" Phillip bit the words through his tight, dry lips.

Clyde wished he was the kind of man who could walk away and leave the man to die the way he deserved. "I will take him on the next train," he stated.

"All I can say is to keep those bandages changed. The infection is bad now."

"All right, Doc, I will tend to it. I will need a wheeled chair for him," Clyde said.

The doctor pushed a chair into the room and gave Phillip a bottle of laudanum. "Drink up, man. If it don't kill you, you will wish it had when the pain gets to you."

Phillip drained the bottle and wiped his mouth with the back of his filthy hand. Clyde wrapped his arms around the disgusting human and carried him to the wheelchair and then to a bath house to make him presentable to begin the ride home.

*****

Gracie read the telegram from her father again.

Bringing Phillip home on Tuesday afternoon train. Alive.

She blinked hard and shoved it back into her apron pocket. Her mother worked in a frenzy. The kitchen was already clean, but she scrubbed the table again. "Gracie, you and the kids will stay with us. He will, too, of course. I can't see you being off at your farm alone with him. I won't allow it. You and the young'uns can't be alone with him. Are you hearing me, Gracie? You are still healing. You can't do this alone. Are you afraid of him?"

Gracie let her mother's words trail through the morning without comprehension. Word had already spread through town that Phillip was coming home to Trinidad.

Gracie felt her body turn to stone. *What will he do to me? Will he kill me for running away?*

Chapter 34

Mrs. Langley knocked on the door of her long-time boarder. She heard movement in the room and urged, "Mary, there is a man here to see you."

The door creaked open and Mrs. Langley drew in a sharp breath. She had never seen Mary Dewey in any kind of garb except for the plainest fabrics available. The blue calico brought out the color of her eyes. She noted the high color in Mary's cheeks. *Why, she is almost pretty!*

"Thank you Mrs. Langley," Mary said as she passed through the door and into the wide hallway.

"Your man friend is quite handsome, Mary."

"Man friend?"

"Of course, he brought flowers."

"Flowers?" she remarked as she noted the daisies in his large hand.

John shifted uneasily from one foot to the other and slurred his words, "I hope you like flowers."

"I don't know. I never had any before."

He flashed a quick, nervous smile, revealing even teeth. A lock of his curly black hair tumbled to his tanned forehead. His dark brown eyes sparkled. He said, "Mrs. Dewey, it is my pleasure to offer this humble offering of flowers to you this evening."

"Thank you kindly," she said as the color deepened in her cheeks.

"Are you ready to dine?"

"Yes, thank you."

He offered his arm and she took it. She held the daisies and fumbled with them. "Mary, let me take them and put them in some water for you. I will leave them here in the entry for you and you can take them to your room when you get back home," Mrs. Langley offered.

The walk to the restaurant was short. The waiter seated them in a quiet corner and they looked at the menu. John looked over the top of the menu at Mary and suggested, "The roast beef dinner sounds good."

"Yes, it does, Mr. Forrester."

"I would like for you to call me John."

"Oh."

"May I call you Mary? It is my intention to become friends, or maybe even more if you would consider it."

She coughed quietly and asked, "Yes, John, but why would you pursue me?"

"The more I thought about you, the more I knew that I wanted to know you better. You are what people call a 'straight shooter'. You tell the truth and don't bother with flattery. I felt from the start that I could trust you to be honest with me."

"Have women been dishonest with you in the past?"

"To be completely truthful, I have never had a woman friend."

The waiter returned to take their order. John ordered the roast beef plate for both of them.

Mary leaned back in the plush chair and allowed herself to enjoy being taken care of.

"It has been a long time since anyone...ah...took me to eat at such a nice place. Honestly, I have never seen the inside of a place so nice as this," she said.

"I would like to take care of you...," his voice trailed off and he blushed.

Mary looked down at her hands and said, "No one ever said that kind of thing to me before."

"I am not good with words, but I do want to tell you that you are pretty tonight."

Her eyebrows shot up almost as quickly as tears sprang into her eyes. The waiter brought their dinner and each was quiet through the first few mouthfuls of the savory food. "Forgive me, I meant to say 'thank you'. I am not accustomed to hearing things like that," she said quietly.

"I don't think I have ever said those words myself," he said, and burst into uneasy laughter.

Mary laughed with him and shook her head, saying, "We are a mess, aren't we?"

"Guilty as charged, madam."

"I think we should stop trying to say things we are not accustomed to saying and try to be at ease with one another."

"I would agree, Mary, but my heart is full. I want to say things to you that I have never said before. I have never been in love before." He noticed the startled look in her eyes.

"Yes, I think I have strong feelings of love for you. Thinking about you makes me happy. I hope that one day you might think fondly of me, too."

"I...ah..."

"Mary, you don't have to answer my bold statement. I just told you so that you would know that I am serious about getting to know you. Let's finish our meal and speak of less weighty subjects."

"Okay."

"This is wonderful food, isn't it?"

"Yes."

"Where do you take your meals most of the time, that is, when you are home in Denver?"

"Meals are provided with the room at Mrs. Langley's."

"Good food?"

"Good enough for me. She is a good friend to me."

He swallowed a bite of the warm mashed potatoes. "Where do you go to speak next?"

She shook her head and dabbed her mouth with her white linen napkin. "I don't go anywhere to speak anymore. Trinidad was the last time. I decided that I caused more trouble when I shared my message than I should have."

"What will you do for money? I mean, it is none of my business. I am sorry."

"My son has sent me a small allowance for years. It is enough for my keep."

"Still, it must be hard. You have traveled for so many years with your message."

"It was time to stop. I am tired."

"I see."

She took another bite of beef and contemplated her next words. "It is not glamorous work. There has always been controversy about my speaking. I have slept in some of the most uncomfortable places. The food was sparse, at best. No, money was not a reason for the travel. In fact, I may be better off without the speaking work."

"That is a shame. I can see where your message could be of great value to many people," he said.

"I did it in obedience to the Lord."

The waiter interrupted them, "Would you like some of our dessert? Our specialty tonight is bread pudding."

"I would love some, and get a serving for the pretty lady, also," John said.

They lingered over the bread pudding and walked slowly down the street to the boarding house. When they reached the porch, he took her hand and blinked quickly. "Mary, I would like to kiss you goodbye. Would that be all right?"

"Ah, yes, I suppose."

He bent down to reach her upturned face. His lips brushed hers lightly. He gave her a slight hug and tipped his hat. "I will be back in a few weeks. That is, if you will see me again."

"Yes. That is...that would be nice."

"I would stay a few days, but I am saving up money to get a home.

I can't ask a woman to be my bride if I don't have a home for her." He turned and sprinted down the street. After a few paces, he wheeled around and yelled, "I love you, Mary."

She felt a warm sensation from her toes to the top of her head as she stared down the street until he was out of sight.

Chapter 35

"Get your lazy bones over here! I want out of this bed right now!" Phillip yelled.

Gracie trotted into the room and pushed the wheelchair up to the bed. She reached to help him and he wrenched her arm from her shoulder socket. She muffled a scream.

"There, there, Gracie. It ain't like your arm got cut off or anything."

Her eyes widened as she backed away from him and watched as he grabbed the wheelchair with his powerful arms and maneuvered into it in one quick motion.

"Ain't it somethin' that I didn't die? Aren't you just so happy that you ain't a widow?"

She covered her mouth with her hand to stifle a sob.

"Wait, I heard that you had a replacement for me already. You didn't waste any time, did you?"

"No...I...ah..."

"Yes, siree, I heard about Timothy Forrester. He swooped in pretty fast, didn't he?"

Sweat trickled down the back of her neck. She gasped, "I don't know what you are talking about."

His eyes narrowed as he pushed against her legs with his wheelchair. He sneered, "My poker buddies filled me in. Don't think that you have any secrets from me."

"I swear I don't have secrets!" she croaked.

He saw the blue flame of terror in her eyes and a wicked smile spread across his rough face. Taking her pale hand in his, he gave it an exaggerated kiss. "I'm starving. Does your ma have breakfast ready yet?"

"Yes."

"Take me in there, then!" he yelled.

Emily Randall dropped the dish into place at the sound of his voice. Her heart jumped into her throat when she saw the ashen face of her daughter. *How much more of this treatment can Gracie take?*

"Good morning, Ma," Phillip said in a mocking voice.

Emily nodded in his direction.

"What's the matter? Did you lose your voice? I told you, 'good morning'!"

"Phillip!" Gracie charged.

He swung around in the chair and pushed her to the floor. Gracie banged her head on the table on the way down. Blood spurted from her nose and down the front of her dress.

"Shame on you, Phillip!" Emily scolded.

Standing, Gracie grabbed a dishrag and staunched the bleeding from her nose. She stumbled to the back door of the kitchen and plunged through it, out to the porch. The pounding of her head kept time with her feet. She half-ran, half-walked out of the yard and continued aimlessly to the edge of town.

Timothy saw her before she saw him. She was in sad shape.

Her hair was wild. He ran to her. "What happened?" he gasped.

She shook her head. "I can't...say...anything."

"You are bleeding!"

"Just my nose."

He touched her temple and traced a large lump. "Phillip!"

She turned her head away and sobbed. "I have to go back."

"No!"

"My babies are there!" she yelled.

He put his arm around her shoulders and led her to the livery stable. "Uncle John will have some horse medicine. It will help those bruises and scrapes. We need to take care of your nosebleed, too."

She felt numb and didn't have the strength to resist.

The smell of fresh hay and leather was the first sensation she noticed as they walked through the wide door. He was glad that he had cleaned up the place for Uncle John while he was gone on his trip to Denver.

He opened the door to his uncle's quarters and pulled out the only chair for her. He strode over to the stove and saw the water he heated to wash dishes. *Good thing I didn't wash those plates this morning.* It was still somewhat warm from its initial heating. He grabbed a clean rag from a bundle of rags that was kept for doctoring horses and dipped it into the water.

After squeezing it out for her, he stepped over to Gracie and carefully touched it to her temple.

She jumped as if he were a rattlesnake. "I won't hurt you. Let me help you." He noted the blank look on her tear-streaked face. "This happen a lot?" he whispered the question.

She turned her head so that he couldn't read her eyes. He knelt down before her and sopped up the blood streaks from her face. He returned to the stove and rinsed out the rag. The horse medicine was easily within reach. Grabbing it up, he opened the square lid on the red and yellow tin box. When his index finger was loaded with the golden glob of medicine, he came close to her. The bruise on the side of her head had grown dark red and blue. He started when he saw that the white of her left eye was blood-red. "He hit you hard!"

"I fell against the table before I hit the floor," she stated flatly.

He blew air through his teeth to keep from cursing as he gingerly applied the balm to her wounds. When the ministrations were over, he placed his hands on her shoulders and pulled her close to him. She laid her head on his chest, just below his chin. He smoothed the wild curls that tickled his nose and turned her face to him. She was a beautiful, wounded girl.

His warm lips caressed her broken mouth in a tender kiss. It was better medicine to her soul than the ointment. She closed her eyes tight and memorized the sweetness of the moment.

Then she pressed her hands to his chest and pushed him away.

"I am married. It doesn't matter how he treats me. I made a vow to God."

He stood and turned his back away from her. "Forgive me. I...just...to see you like this. I have to tell you ... so that you know ...that someone loves you, no matter what!" Tears filled his eyes and he grabbed his face with his hands. "It tears me up to see you with that monster!"

She stood carefully and moved out of the little room into the stable. "I have to go home."

"Let me take you."

"He might kill me if he saw me with you." She left him standing in the darkness of the stable.

He fell to his knees and reached up toward the ceiling, crying aloud, "God, why do you let people suffer like this?" Scenes from his childhood blazed through his tortured mind. "I can't stand it if she has to suffer. Deliver her...somehow."

He repeated the prayer over and over.

Chapter 36

John found Timothy asleep on the old cot in the living quarters. Somehow, Tim looked like a little boy again. Was it the sadness that tugged at the corners of his mouth or the long sigh in his sleep? He put his big hand on the young man's shoulder and shook it gently.

"Tim, I'm back. Is everything all right?"

Timothy blinked his eyes. The sun streamed through the one small window near the bed.

"Sorry, I ...I...shouldn't be asleep in the middle of the day."

John studied his nephew's face. "No bother. What is going on?"

"It's...Gracie...I think she is in danger."

"Son, Gracie is another man's wife. She is not your concern."

Balling up his fists, he jerked out of the bed. "He's the one! He hurts her!"

"A man has a right to treat his wife as he sees fit. It isn't good, but it is the way things are."

"If you had seen her today...the blood...her face...You wouldn't say that! I love her!" he cried.

Slowly, John put his arm around the trembling young man. "It's the law, son. You would be in the wrong if you interfered with a man and his wife. I think you need to go on back to the ranch and put some distance between you and Gracie. You can't be taking up with another man's wife, no matter how he treats her."

Timothy grabbed his hat, went into the stable and saddled his horse. John waited a few minutes before he followed him. "These things have a way of working out. Phillip is mean since he lost his legs. One day, he will come to grips with life as it is and the anger will subside."

"You and I both know better than that. We lived for years with a man that let anger rule him. He nearly killed me many times. Even though I forgave him, I still remember the pain of his fists. I don't want that for Gracie."

"I know it don't sound like much, but we can pray for her...and him...that things will get better. You can't have her. You know that, don't you?"

"I know. I swear I won't stop myself from killing him if he hurts her again." Timothy gave Butterscotch a kick and loped through the town. He urged him into a full run all the way to the Young's ranch.

Ralph yelled at him as he skidded to a stop at the barn, "You will kill that horse running him like that! You done run him to the ground. He's all lathered up!"

Timothy pushed past him and took his mount into the barn and pulled the saddle and blanket off. Foam dripped off the animal. He snorted loudly. Timothy pulled on the bridle and walked him out of the barn and around the acreage beside the house. Slowly Butterscotch cooled down. After sufficient time had passed, Timothy led him to the stall and began carefully brushing him down next to the water trough. The horse took his fill of water. Timothy gave him a little hay and went light on the oats. "I'm sorry, boy. I should be whipped for treating you like that!" he said in true repentance. He placed his forehead on the buckskin's neck. "I'm so sorry."

The horse continued eating the fresh hay. He turned away from his master and swished his tail into Timothy's face. "I would be mad, too. I will make it up to you."

Timothy went to his room and paced the floor. "Gracie, why did you marry that brute?"

A sharp knock sounded on the wooden plank door. "Timothy, I need to talk with you."

"Come in."

Ted opened the door and faced Timothy. "You are a better horseman than that! What is the story?" he asked.

Timothy drew his mouth into a firm line. "It won't happen again. I wasn't thinking."

"I know there is more to it than that. It isn't your nature to be cruel."

"That's the last thing I want to be! I have seen too much suffering! I hate that I made my horse suffer!"

Ted's answer came softer, "Boy, you have to tell me what is going on."

The tenderness of his friend's voice broke him. A loud sob escaped from his throat. "I think Gracie's husband is going to kill her. I can't let that happen."

Ted sat on the cot and studied the floor boards. "I don't know. How can you keep her safe from her husband? She belongs to him."

Timothy's face burned hot. He yelled, "That is the kind of things people said while Pa beat the living daylights out of me and starved me and told me he was going to kill me. He said it in front of people. Nobody stuck up for me until Uncle John helped me escape."

"I know."

"I don't want her to die. I ...love her."

"I know."

Timothy's head jerked up in alarm. "Is it that obvious? Does everyone know?" he asked.

"Pretty obvious."

He blew out a slow breath. "Then I better keep away from town. Phillip will calm down if he doesn't see me around. It is probably my fault that he is angry if it is that obvious."

"That is probably the best move you can make right now."

"I guess you are right."

"Tim, I need you to round up strays in the summer pasture.

Our count was down yesterday and I fear there may be a big cat or wolves taking down the calves."

Timothy nodded, "I will need a fresh mount. Give me a few minutes to get my gear together for the trip."

"Take Scout. He is sure-footed."

"...Be seeing you in a few days, then."

"God's speed," Ted said as he turned on his heel and left Timothy to ready himself for a few solitary days.

Chapter 37

Mary found a letter sitting next to her plate at the supper table. Mrs. Langley smiled at her and asked, "Is this from your beau?"

Redness crept up her neck and onto her cheeks. Mary ducked her head and said, "Yes."

"I imagine you will be leaving us soon."

"Mrs. Langley?"

"Of course you will be moving to Trinidad. That is obvious."

"He hasn't asked me."

Mrs. Langley chuckled as she took a sip of coffee.

"Excuse me," Mary said as she took her letter and slipped up the stairs.

Once in her room, she opened the creamy envelope and read the simple lettering on the sheet of fresh paper.

Mary,

I want to see you again on August 11. Could I have the pleasure of your company for supper? There is an important question that I am gathering my nerve up to ask you. Begin forming your answer before we meet. I have purchased a small cottage on the edge of town. I need to know your favorite colors. What do you think for the kitchen, parlor, and bedroom? I want to prepare it for my bride. You can guess what my question will be, can't you?

With all the love in my heart,
John Forrester

She gasped as tears trickled down her cheeks. *Yes! John, the answer is 'yes'!* Her mind raced. *He really loves me? He bought a house?*

Mary Dewey fairly ran to the telegraph office. The busy clerk gave her a withering look. "Can I help you, Ma'am?" he asked.

"I want to send a telegram to Trinidad, Colorado. The name is John Forrester."

"What would be the content of the message?" he asked.

"Yes."

"'Yes', what?"

"Just...'yes'", she answered.

*****

John finished a hurried noon meal at the pie shop. When he stepped onto the boardwalk, a young boy ran up to him, saying, "Mr. Forrester, telegram."

"Thank you, son."

He opened the telegram and read the reply. "Yippee!" he whooped.

His mind raced as he trotted to the nearby general store. "Can I help you?" the clerk asked.

"Yes sir, I am in need of a wedding dress."

"You? Really?"

He shook his head, laughing, "No, not me but for my bride."

"I have some pretty dresses here for her to choose from. Tell her to come by and make her choice."

"She doesn't live here. I know that she wouldn't get anything that she is worthy of. She is the most wonderful woman I have ever met. There is nothing too good for her."

"I see."

"Where are they? I want to have a look."

"Right this way," the man said as he led him to the front of the store. "This one came in last week. It is very impractical. Not many women in these parts would purchase it. I don't even know why it came in the order."

Sweat stood out on his forehead. He had never considered the look of a dress. The one that the clerk indicated was like nothing he had ever seen. "What is it made out of?" he asked in a low voice.

"That is silk."

"I would say that the color is sort of the color of wine. Is that right?"

The man grinned. "I heard one woman say that it was wine-red."

"Her golden hair would show out pretty in this."

"Look at the back. There is a bustle all gathered in the back."

"What on earth is that for?" John marveled.

A young woman entered from the back room.

She observed the men for a moment and said, "Papa, you don't know beans about women's clothing. What are you doing?"

"He is in the market for a weddin' dress...fer his bride."

"Let me show you the detail of the dress." She continued without waiting for permission from the astonished gentlemen. "It is made of silk. The high neckline is accented with buttons covered with matching lace. Leg-of-lamb sleeves..."

"Leg of lamb?" John asked.

"That is what you call that puffed sleeve that goes into a narrow straight sleeve from the middle of the upper arm to the wrist. May I continue?"

"Please..." he said.

"You will notice that more buttons fasten the sleeves from the forearm clear down to the wrists. The bodice is covered with silk lace."

John didn't know what a 'bodice' was until she pointed to the area from the waist and above. *This is complicated.*

"The full skirt is enhanced by the swoop of a swatch of lace that pulls across the front of the dress and meets in the back into a full bustle. It is the latest fashion!" her voice gained momentum up to the crescendo at the end.

"Bravo, daughter! That is stringing together some fancy words," the clerk said.

John cleared his throat and asked, "Then, it is appropriate for a wedding dress?"

"It would make a lovely wedding dress. Of course, you will need to get some dressy shoes. She couldn't wear the old clunky work shoes the women around here wear with something as pretty as this."

"Shoes? Do you have some?"

She frowned and said, "She would need to try them on...it is too bad that you can't take her to a big city like Denver. I am sure they would have something pretty for the dress."

"She lives in Denver. I can take her to get shoes the day of the wedding."

The girl was caught up in the excitement of this unknown woman's wedding. She studied the contents of her display case and found a large cameo brooch. "Look how this sets off the beauty of the dress."

"Is it expensive?" he asked.

"It is two dollars. The dress is fifteen."

"I have it."

"Good. If I may make a suggestion?"

"Yes."

"Go next door and show the milliner the dress. She will be able to help you get a matching hat for it."

"Thank you so much."

"Did you get the wedding ring?" she asked.

"No, I forgot."

"There is a pretty golden band. If it doesn't fit right, we can get it sized."

He paid her the money for all the items and considered his shopping trip a success.

Now I just have to figure out the nonsense of a fancy hat! Cecil would laugh his head off if he could see me now.

Chapter 38

Mary stood in front of the mirror. She had never seen such a pretty dress. Mrs. Langley had invited Gertie Long, a former boarder, to come in and assist Mary.

"Gertie! You look wonderful! How are the doctor and your baby?"

"Jim is minding William downstairs while we get you ready for your wedding. You look so pretty. I love that dress."

"It is good of you to come."

"I wouldn't miss your wedding for the world. You were very good to me when I boarded here."

"Thank you."

Mary brushed her long, blond hair. Her hands shook as she attempted to pin it into place on the top of her head.

"Mary, would you mind if I help you dress your hair?" Gertie asked.

"Would you?"

"Mrs. Langley, do you have a curling iron we can use?"

Presently, Mrs. Langley produced the curling iron and lit the coal oil lamp on the small table in the room. She placed the barrel of the device in the chimney next to the flame.

Gertie allowed it to heat for a minute and maneuvered it through locks of Mary's hair again and again after each heating.

The results were stunning. Spiraling curls framed her face. Most of her heavy hair was twisted into a large chignon at the nape of her neck. A few locks of hair were reserved to trail down her left shoulder in long curls.

Mary held the mirror in her hand and covered her mouth. "I don't even look like myself. I...look...almost pretty!" she exclaimed.

"You are a beautiful bride. Look how your eyes shine. Gertie done up your hair really pretty. You still have a trim figure. Mary, you should hold your head up high. You are a real lady, " Mrs. Langley said.

Gertie placed the filmy hat on the crown of her shiny golden hair. The burgundy satin cap was small with a point that rested on the top of her forehead and followed the contour of her head. A netted veil fell down the front of her face and tucked under her chin, gathering in the back and cascading down her back with a puff of matching ostrich feathers.

Mrs. Langley and Gertie came down the stairs to Jim and John. "You men folk, go on to the church. We don't want John to see his bride before the ceremony."

"If you will be coming right along, I will take baby William with me," Jim said.

"We will be there moments after you, darling," Gertie said.

After the men left the house, the rest of the boarders stood in the parlor and watched as the bride entered the room. She hugged each of them. Tears stood in their eyes. "God be with you, dear friends."

"God be with you, Mary."

*****

The church was mostly empty. The pastor, bride, groom, Mrs. Langley, Gertie, and Jim Long with William, were there to celebrate the occasion with them. Mary was delirious as she looked into John's eyes.

"Have you heard back from your son...Sam? Is he coming?" John asked quietly.

Mary shook her head. "He sent a telegram. He and Clementine will not be attending today. I didn't expect that they would come," she said with a catch in her throat.

"I want to make you happy, Mary. He will come around someday."

"I hope you are right but if I have you, that is better than enough for me," she said.

A crowded sanctuary was not necessary when she had a man like him. She blinked quickly to keep her tears at bay. She offered him a brilliant smile. The joy she felt lit her face with a soft glow. His smile matched hers.

"We are gathered together before God and this company, to join this man and this woman in holy matrimony. Marriage is a matter that should be entered into with gravity and great care. It is a commitment for a lifetime. John Forrester, do you take Mary Dewey to be your lawfully, wedded wife?"

"I do."

"Mary Dewey, do you take John Forrester to be your lawfully, wedded husband?"

"I do."

John heard the rest of the charge from the pastor and it made his heart quicken. He was responsible for another person. Her happiness depended on him. Was he up to it? He looked into her sparkling brown eyes and knew that he would do everything he could to make her life the best it could be.

"I now pronounce that you are husband and wife. You may kiss your bride."

Chapter 39

Timothy waited for the train from Denver to arrive. He could hardly wait to see his uncle. It was a good thing that at least someone he loved was happy. There had been a bit of work left to do in finishing up the house so he had stayed behind to do the work. He had opened the windows so that it would be as cool as possible for the summer weather. The position of the windows made for a good cross-breeze.

That bright little house is quite a departure from the dreary quarters Uncle John has lived in all of his life. Who would have thought how a color like yellow could brighten up a little kitchen? Nan Young and her girls placed fresh flowers on the kitchen table for Mary. The smell from the bouquet wafted throughout the house.

He heard the train whistle moments before he saw the train. Several passengers disembarked ahead of the newlyweds. Timothy almost didn't recognize them. Their faces were wreathed in smiles. He had never seen such a happy couple. Mary wore the dress that Uncle John bought her for the wedding. She didn't even look like the plain woman he had first met. He had heard that being loved could bring out the beauty in anyone. Now he believed it.

Uncle John spotted Timothy and wrapped his arms around him in a strong bear hug.

Timothy shook Mary's hand shyly. "Hello, Mary...Aunt Mary," he said.

"It is good to see you, Timothy."

The greeting was cut short by loud shouts in the street. "You can't tell me that the brat you are carrying is mine! Gracie, come face me! I ought to kill you right where you stand. If you don't get out of that store, I will come in and shoot up the whole place! Do you hear me, woman?"

Gracie stepped out of the general store and into the street. Clyde and Emily followed their daughter and stood close by. Gracie handed baby Hope to her mother while Wayne clung to his grandfather's hand. Gracie stepped closer to her husband.

He brandished the gun and screamed at her, "That unborn baby is not mine!"

"What are you talking about?" she asked in a low, calming voice.

"You can't fool me. At the poker game last night, Frank told me he saw you with Timothy Forrester. You are already showing," he sneered.

"You are the father of all of my babies, even the one I am expecting!" she yelled.

The sheriff pushed his way through the gathering crowd. The sound of his boots stomping the boardwalk rang through the air. "Phillip, put that gun down. This is something that should be handled in private. You don't want the whole town knowing your business," he stated forcefully.

Phillip turned in the wheelchair and looked over his shoulder at the lawman.

In doing so, he almost fell out of the chair. His mind was fuzzy from the whiskey he had drunk since the poker game. His eyes rested on Timothy, whose attention was directed to the loud commotion. "What do you say to this, Tim?" he slurred.

"Gracie is your wife," Timothy said.

"Ole Frank saw you taking her into the stable. That don't sound right to me," he said as he loaded the six-shooter that he took up from his lap.

Timothy edged closer to Phillip. "I saw her bleeding. She was stumbling down the street. I put medicine on her wounds. That is all," he said as color flooded his face.

"That's right, Phillip," Gracie said.

Phillip's attention directed toward Gracie. He contorted his face as he took aim at her heart. Sheriff Moore rushed toward the man. Clyde dove in front of his daughter. The gun blasted. Clyde cried out in agony. The bullet hit him in the heart. Gracie knelt down beside her father, screaming, "Pa, Pa, don't die! Do you hear me? Don't die! We need you!"

Clyde opened his mouth to speak to his daughter, but death captured him. Emily laid her head on his chest not mindful of the blood flowing from the wounds. "Don't leave me!" she sobbed, "I have loved you all of my life."

Sheriff Moore grabbed the weapon from the crazed man's grasp. "You are under arrest. You killed a man."

Gracie looked from her father's still face to the hateful countenance of her husband. She reached for her little boy and pulled him close to her. Great wracking sobs shook her body. Phillip yelled as he was taken to the jail, "I'm glad I killed him. Only thing is, I wish it was you!"

Wayne rubbed his mama's head clumsily and lisped, "Mama, Pampaw is sleeping."

She looked into his innocent blue eyes. How would she comfort this child? She opened her mouth to speak, but no words came out.

Timothy took a step toward her and John grabbed him by the shoulder. He stopped short. "Tim, keep your distance. You don't want to make things worse for her do you?" he asked quietly.

Timothy hung his head and remained in the background while two men gathered Clyde up and took him to the undertaker's parlor. After he was taken, Pastor Reynolds escorted Emily, Gracie, and the children to their home.

Mary approached Timothy. He saw his sorrow reflected in her eyes. "Come with us," she said.

John took the small trunk belonging to Mary that the porter had deposited at his feet. They walked to the little house without a word. Once inside, Mary doffed her hat and asked, "John, where is the bedroom? I need to change and make us a good meal."

He led her to the room and put the trunk next to the bed. "There you go," he said as he walked out the door to speak with his nephew.

"I am sorry. This is your first day in your home. I need to go," Timothy said.

"Mary understands. Let us help you get through this."

Timothy paced the floor, "He killed Clyde! His aim was to kill Gracie! Do you see that the man is a monster?"

"I know he is. It is a good thing he is in jail."

"I have to see Gracie!"

"Stay put. You heard the accusations Phillip flung out in front of the whole town. If you go to help her now, the town gossips will never stop wagging their tongues."

"I don't care!" Timothy exclaimed.

John grabbed hold of Timothy's forearm and urged, "You may not care, but a woman has a lot to lose when the winds of gossip ravage her. Think of the children. It is going to be hard enough on them the way it is."

Mary joined them in the kitchen. "Let me go and offer my sympathy to them. I will let Gracie know that you wish to be with her but don't want to cause her more trouble."

"Could you give her a note from me?" Timothy asked.

"Of course," she said.

John found a scrap of brown paper that the dry goods store wrapped one of his recent purchases in. He extended it to Timothy with a nub of a pencil and said, "This is all I have in the way of writing materials."

"Thank you, it'll do," Timothy said as he took them to the small table in the corner of the kitchen. After painstakingly scrawling a message, he handed it to Mary.

*****

Pastor Reynolds opened the door a crack. "Mary Dewey, is that you?" he asked.

"Yes...well...I am Mary Forrester now. I came to speak with Gracie and her mother, if I may."

He opened the door widely so that she could walk through. Mary spotted Emily sitting in a rocker, holding baby Hope. Beth Reynolds, the pastor's wife, sat close to her.

Gracie blinked her eyes in disbelief, "Mary, is that you? It is kind of you to come. Mother, Mary helped me when I ran away from Phillip. She was on the train and took care of me as if I were her own child," she said as tears made rivers down her face.

Emily stood and handed Hope to Beth. She wrapped her arms around Mary and spoke in a voice barely above a whisper. "I can never thank you enough for what you did for my girl...and Hope."

Mary patted the distressed woman on the back and stepped out of her embrace. She reached into her pocket and grasped a folded piece of rough paper, giving to Gracie, "I have a note from Timothy.

He wants you to know that he is sorry for your trouble," Mary stopped and whispered, indicating Emily, "How is your mother holding up?"

"Numb...just like me."

"I am so sorry. It is obvious that your pa loved you a lot. He saved your life. There is no greater love than this that a man lay down his life for another."

"My poor papa!"

Mary folded the girl in her strong arms and prayed that the Lord would give the mother and daughter strength to get through the sorrow. She stood beside the table next to little Wayne and ruffled his hair. He looked up from his cup of milk and grinned at her. She barely made out his gibberish, "Pam paw is sleepin'."

"Yes, sweetheart, he was a good man."

She put her hand on Emily's back and leaned in for a gentle hug. The woman gave her a brief smile. "I will be back to check on you. Do you have anything for supper?"

"I...ah...haven't thought of that," Gracie said.

"Will you allow me to bring something for you this evening?" Mary asked.

"Thank you, yes," Gracie said, sighing. "I just can't keep my thoughts in line...now."

Mary approached the pastor and spoke softly, "Will the church folk see to them?"

Pastor Reynolds gave her a sad look and said, "It is hard to say.

Those who would believe the worst of little Gracie might hold the others back from ministering to them with kindness."

"I won't forsake them. I promise."

"That is good news, Mrs. Dew...I mean...Mrs. Forrester. God bless you. We must be going soon. I am happy that you are bringing them some supper." Mary bid them 'goodbye' to walk the few blocks to her new home.

"Beth, we need to be going, too. Mrs. Randall, we will be back first thing tomorrow to tend to the funeral," Pastor Reynolds said as he opened the door and let his sweet-faced wife out. He paused and then followed her, shutting the door carefully.

Gracie picked up the heavy, brown paper and slowly unfolded it. She recognized the writing.

Gracie,

I am so sad about your pa. He was a good man. I could not believe that Phillip intended to shoot you. I am glad your life was spared. I know you are sad, but your little children need their ma. I never knew mine and I can't help but think that if I had known her, things would have been a lot better for me. I will help you as much as I can. I am told that it would hurt your reputation if I come to see you. Know this, if you ever need me to be there, I will come. - Timothy

She stared at the writing for an hour before the words made any sense to her. Her mind was tired. It was good that he would not be coming to see her.

She didn't know how she was supposed to feel right now. *Papa is dead! He died for me...he saved my life...my life! Because of me, he is dead! If I hadn't run away from Phillip in California...* She paced the floor wringing her hands.

Emily stood and placed Hope in her cradle. She gathered Gracie in her arms. Gracie sobbed. Emily moaned and swayed with her daughter. "I love you, sweetie. Everything will work out. We will be all right. We just have to get through the funeral," Emily soothed.

"Oh, Mama!"

"We have to think of Wayne and Hope. We must press on."

Chapter 40

The courthouse was full, almost as full as the church was for the funeral for Clyde Randall. It was generally the same crowd, except for a few regulars at the saloon's poker table. Judge Billings was new to the area and had no friends or foes, as yet. He proceeded to the bench as everyone rose to honor him except for the defendant. His face was pinched and angry as he charged the defense attorney, "Your client will stand!"

"He cannot stand because he has no legs."

The statement flustered the judge and he shuffled the papers before him. "You may be seated," he growled.

The stuffy courtroom was quiet except for muffled whispers. Judge Billings cleared his throat loudly. "It appears that everyone saw this man, Phillip Masters, shoot and kill an unarmed man. He is clearly guilty. My duty today is to pronounce the sentence. Will the attorneys state their recommendations?"

Mr. Hines, the lawyer for the prosecution, approached the bench with his statement, "Your Honor, my recommendation is that this cold-blooded murderer be hanged by the neck until dead." He turned on his heel and sat at the table assigned for him in the courtroom.

The attorney for the defense stood next to Phillip in the wheelchair and leveled his gaze at the unfamiliar judge, saying, "Let me introduce myself, I am Robert Cooper and I am here to ask for leniency for this troubled man. As you see, he has no legs. This is a new condition that he finds himself in. Only seven short months ago he and his wife, Gracie, were in California. When he found that she was fleeing the state with his infant child on a train, he embarked upon said transport to compel her not to leave. As he approached her, she pushed him from the doorway and onto the tracks where the vehicle severed his legs from his body."

A gasp from many of the listeners sounded throughout the courtroom. He continued as Phillip sagged in his seat, looking pitiful and helpless, "Phillip Masters was a big, strapping man who could out-work any man he knew. Now he is reduced to...this."

"This brute jumped from the back car to the passenger car where Gracie and her child were sheltered. He missed the landing and fell onto the tracks. I have a witness who can verify this statement to be true," Mr. Hines proclaimed.

Judge Billings looked over his spectacles at Phillip and asked, "Why would he gun down an unarmed man? This crime has no connection with his wife."

"Begging your pardon, Your Honor. The man he killed was his father-in-law.

Because of this, I petition that you send Phillip Masters to prison for the death of Clyde Randall. Thank you."

The judge placed his palms on the big bench where he sat. His face was bland and unreadable. The words he said were clipped and straightforward, "My mind was set to have this man hanged, but seeing that he has been met with misfortune already, I am sentencing him to life in prison at Canon City. That is all. Sheriff, take him away."

Gracie caught her breath when Phillip spotted her in the courtroom and glared at her. Emily shifted Hope to her other side and squeezed Gracie's hand. She held it tightly until Phillip was out of the room. They sat in their seats until the room emptied.

Gracie seemed unaware of the critical looks from many of the crowd. The baby she was expecting kicked her vigorously. She placed her hand on her belly. It would only be another month or two before this one came.

Her eyes met those of her mother. *How am I going to feed another child? How are we going to survive with no money?* She felt panic rise in her throat. A moan escaped as she pulled herself up and locked arms with her mother as they left the courthouse.

John and Mary Forrester waited for them outside on the boardwalk. Emily took Mary's hand, saying, "Thank you for being here. It was good to have you here for us."

Mary stepped over to Gracie and held her in a strong embrace. When she pulled back, she fished an envelope out of her bag. "This is for you. Timothy didn't want me to tell you, but he brought it to me to give to you so your young'uns won't be going without. He said that every time he gets paid, there will be more. He don't want to send it through the mail or deliver it himself because it might cause you trouble."

Tears spilled down Gracie's face. "I don't know what to say. I don't know if I should take it. Is it right to take it, Mary...Mama?" she asked. Her voice was like a small child's.

"We don't have any choice. Mary, tell him we think he is very kind," Emily stated.

Mary shook her head. "He is a good man. I don't believe the gossip and neither does John."

"He is my nephew. I believe his intentions are pure," John said.

"Thank you," Gracie said.

Wayne began crying loudly and Gracie stooped down to console him. "Where did Papa go? He didn't say nothin' to me. Why did he go with the man?" he asked.

"Baby, Papa did something really bad. He went away to be punished," Gracie explained.

"Punished? Did he get punished for shooting that gun? That's when Pam Paw was sleepin'."

Gracie looked into the tearful blue eyes. *He saw it all! This poor baby saw it all!*

She wrapped her arms around him tightly and consoled him, "We will be all right. I promise. Grandma and I will take good care of you and Hope.

*****

Timothy watched from the restaurant across the street from the courthouse. He had requested a table next to the street so that he could observe from behind the lace curtain. He could only imagine what Wayne thought happened on this day and the day of Clyde's death. He wanted to shield all of them from the cruelty of the world, but he couldn't. A few hard-earned dollars would have to do.

He breathed a sigh of relief when Gracie kept the envelope. *That's good. At least they will have food to eat.* He lingered over the meal until Gracie and her family left for home, then he found himself on his uncle's doorstep.

"Hello, Timothy, come on inside!" John exclaimed.

"I need to ask you if you think it would be all right if I went to church tomorrow."

"Why wouldn't you go to church?" he asked.

He rubbed his hands on his thighs in a nervous gesture. "I...ah...probably should go to a different church than Gracie."

"Oh, I see."

"Pastor Reynolds is her pastor. You know...at the little stone church by the creek.

You could go with us to Pastor Morgan's church. He is a good fellow, even though he cut Mary's meetings there short. We have been attending there so that he knows there are no hard feelings. I had already started there before I met Mary. It is a good church. You could stay overnight with us and we could all go together."

"Would that be all right with Mary?"

Mary entered the room with a tray of chocolate cake and cups of milk. "What would be all right with Mary?" she asked. "I baked a cake and brought all of us a piece with some milk. Would that be all right?"

John laughed and rubbed his stomach. "You are bound to make me the fattest man in Trinidad if you keep that up. The good thing is that Timothy will come in a close second since he is staying the night and going to be eating some of your good cookin' tomorrow. He is going to church with us."

"It will take more than a few meals to make you lean gentlemen into fat men. It will be fun trying out my cooking skills on Timothy.

Chapter 41

November blew in with a blizzard. Gracie lay back on her sweat-soaked pillow. The baby that nursed at her breast arrived after two days of torture.

"What are you naming your sweet daughter?" Doctor Johnson asked.

"Emily Jane."

He took her hand and pressed it firmly. Doctor Elmer Johnson was known for his compassion. His words brought her much comfort as he said, "Gracie, things will be better. I think you struggled so much in birthing this child because you have been so distraught with the passing of your father and all the implications of caring for your children on your own. Since Phillip is in prison, your children have been fatherless. The Scripture says that God will be a father to the fatherless. Rest assured that He will never leave you or forsake you. Keep your faith. Everything will work out. I am giving you a sleeping powder to take as soon as she finishes nursing. You must rest. Your mother can care for the children."

"Thank you, Doctor."

He stood in the doorway observing the mother and child. Emily approached him and asked, "Elmer, will you please have some coffee with me?"

"Sure, Emily. It was a long labor."

"Is she going to be all right?"

"She has more strength than you realize."

"Gracie has been through too much for her years."

"So have you."

"Yes," she agreed.

"How are you holding up...about Clyde, I mean?" he asked.

Emily poured two cups of coffee into delicate blue willow china cups. She added a spoon of sugar and stirred. She stared into the black substance and pressed her lips into a determined line. She sighed in spite of her resolve to be strong. She replied, "I am muddling through."

"I have a proposition for you, Emily."

"Really?"

"Would you consider working for me as my nurse? The practice is growing and I am in need of help," he paused and continued, "I would imagine that the money could be of some help to you as well."

"Are you sure?"

"I wouldn't have brought it up if I wasn't sure. Remember, I know you. We went to school together when we were kids. I think you know me well enough to know how I want my patients treated. You would have a kind, but firm way with them."

"Firm?"

"My patients should know that medical orders are to be obeyed."

"Yes...I can see that."

"Now that you understand my position on medical orders, I want you to make sure that Gracie sleeps throughout the day and night. I am sending my sister's daughter, Sally, over to help you with the children so that you can have some rest, also."

"You don't have to do that!"

"Orders, Emily, orders!"

Tears sprang to her eyes. "Thank you," she said.

Chapter 42

The loud banging on the front door sounded like someone was intent on breaking it into splinters. Emily threw it open before more damage could be done. She was not prepared to see Gus Wiley on the other side of the door. The skinny man was stronger than he looked. He held a mostly empty jug of rum in one hand. His bulging, bloodshot eyes looked like black caverns. Tobacco dripped from the corner of his mouth when he opened his mouth to speak, "I wanna...sp..eak...to Phillip's ...woe...man. He nebber give me da deed to...da farm."

"What? Why would he give you that?"

"A bet is a bet."

"A...bet?"

"He lost ...big."

"He lost the farm? You cannot take the farm away from Gracie and her young'uns!" she cried, attempting to shut the door.

He wedged himself between the door jamb and door. "Nope...I...wan it fair..in ..square."

"No."

"The sheriff said that I jist have to tell her an...it would be done."

"We will see about that! Now, get out of here. Gracie is not up to doing business even if she agrees that you won the farm. Come back in two days and we will talk again. Next time you had better be sober!"

He withdrew from the house like the mild mouse of a man everyone knew him to be. *How could Phillip gamble the farm away? That man!*

*****

Sleet pounded the roof as Gracie awoke. She pulled herself up into an upright position and shuffled into the warm kitchen where her mother sat reading her Bible.

Emily looked up with alarm when she heard the approach of her daughter. "What are you doing out of bed? You have another two days left of your confinement!" she exclaimed.

"I am the mother of three children. I can't stay in bed for two weeks, no matter what the tradition is."

"You need to build up your strength."

"I can't let you and Sally do my work for me."

"Sit down, then. I will get you some coffee."

"A storm has blown in. I don't know how you have been able to keep up with the firewood," Gracie said.

"John Forrester and some of the men from the church have been helping with that."

"Oh."

Emily studied Gracie's face and determined that it was time to tell her the hard news about her home. She took a deep breath and kept her voice soft, "Sweetie, I have something bad to tell you. Don't interrupt me. I need to say this all at once or I might not get the facts right.

"Yesterday, Gus Wiley came to lay claim to your farm. It appears that Phillip lost at a game of cards." She held up her hand to still Gracie's questions. "I talked with the sheriff. He says that you have to give him the farm."

"Give him the farm?"

"I do recall that one reason Phillip wanted to marry you so quickly was so that you could file for a homestead next to the land he homesteaded. Papa went with you to file before you were married, so I think you must have filed in your maiden name."

"I remember that. I signed the paper myself."

"You ought to go to a lawyer and find out if Gus can take your homestead. It may be that Phillip didn't change anything after you were married. He could have, but that would be your only chance to save part of it."

Gracie felt like a few boulders were added to the burden she already felt on her back. "I will go see what Mr. Hines says. He is the only attorney I know."

"He will know what to do," Emily said.

*****

Thomas Hines felt anger in the pit of his stomach as he listened to the predicament of the mother of three. He had dealt with many scoundrels and he was certain that Phillip Masters was one of the lowest of the low.

"Did you go to the land title office and look at your deed?"

She fingered her bag nervously and was barely audible, "No, sir."

His heart jerked. "Let's go take a look at exactly what you have. There may be a way around it so that you can at least keep half of the land."

She followed him to the land office. The clerk produced the paperwork they requested and found that Phillip had not taken the time to change her one hundred sixty acres into his name. Mr. Hines noted that the first five years were already almost up.

"Mrs. Masters, have you done any improvements on your portion of the land?"

"Our house is on this acreage because it is near the creek and we planted some potatoes and other vegetables."

"We can file for a deed of title if you can submit proof of residence and proof of the improvements. Let's go to my office and finish this discussion there."

After Gracie settled in the seat across from her lawyer, she felt some hope rising.

"Mrs. Masters, you will need to file for a divorce from Mr. Masters before you can save your land."

"Divorce?"

"You will have to give Gus Hines the land that Phillip gambled, but if you are divorced from him, Gus will have no claim on your land."

"Do you realize that you are asking a hard thing? My children and I will be outcasts! People don't cotton to a divorced woman or her children."

He leaned back in his chair and studied her face carefully. "If you don't divorce this man, he may gamble away everything you have...even in prison. You need to sever all ties to him legally, so that you can give your children a life. Right now, you have this land. There will be a day that he will gamble it away when he finds out that Gus didn't get his hands on it. It is my guess that the man has no heart for you or his children. You will have to face the gossips and make as good a life as you can with the little that you have. You could even sell out and start over somewhere else," he said.

"I have little money to pay you for your services."

"Sometimes having a good conscience is good enough. Just knowing that I could help you and your children get away from this situation helps me remember why I became a lawyer."

Chapter 43

Timothy chased a wayward calf out of a tangle of greasewood brush. The Sangre De Cristo Mountain Range stood as a framework against the cold winter sky. He had been looking for this calf and his mama for the better part of the day. Ted had told him to scour the area and bring them closer to home to finish the winter. Grass was on the verge of being overgrazed and the rest of the herd had made it to the winter pasture. It was a small box canyon that provided shelter from harsh weather. Being a sight closer to the headquarters of the ranch also made for better care for the animals. Of course, there were a few ornery critters that seemed to not know what was best for them. Timothy reasoned that he owed his job to those rebellious cattle. Without them there would be little for him to do, with the exception of riding fence. Every cowhand hated that particular job.

He hunkered down into the sheepskin coat and tied his felt cowboy hat down over his ears with his large blue bandana. Good thing the other cowpokes weren't with him, else they would make sport of him. He shrugged off the idea because he dearly hated earaches. Keeping the wind out of his ears was the only way to spare himself that displeasure.

Eventually the stubborn cow and calf were joined with the herd in the protected area. Timothy was at their heels. Ralph spotted the man and pointed to the campfire. Timothy rode past him to the place where the horses were staked out, swung his leg over his mount and secured him. He pulled off the saddle, saddle bags, and bedroll. Searching in his gear, he measured out a few oats, placing them in his hat. "Here you go, Butterscotch. You are a good boy."

Ralph approached him with a steaming cup of coffee. He gave him a measured look and remarked, "You don't look any worse for wear."

"They weren't that hard to find. That cow just has a mind of her own. How are you faring?"

"Fair 'nuff."

"Looks like you and the boys got 'em all."

"Yep."

Timothy took a gulp of the coffee and fairly spat the words, "This is vile stuff!"

"Jist like I like it," Ralph said with a grin.

One by one, the stars lit up the sky. No clouds. That was a good sign. The moon looked close enough to touch. Timothy could never get used to the brilliant western night sky. "Have you ever been to Texas or Montana?" He didn't really realize that he had said his thought out loud.

"Those two places are horses of different colors. In Texas, it depends on where in that big old place you hang your hat. Montana is a lot like Colorado. What are you thinkin', kid?"

"Haven't you ever wanted your own place?"

"I have everything I need here on the ranch," Ralph answered.

Timothy placed his hat on his head and moved toward the fire. The warmth felt good. "It is better camping here...not in the weather so bad," he said, trying to change the subject.

"There are places in Texas where it doesn't get cold...ever."

"I've heard that."

"They round up longhorn there. They are free for the finding. You just have to get them to Dodge City, Kansas. Are you thinking of that?" Ralph asked.

"I don't know. It is a thought. I will have to study out where Dodge City is and if it is something I think I can do. Don't you have to belong to an outfit?"

"As few as twelve men can drive two thousand cattle. You would have to find men you could trust to hold the line and not balk on you," Ralph said as he massaged the stubble on his chin.

"You know the reason why I need to leave here. I can't be this close to Gracie and not talk to her. It kills me the way people talk about her. I know she can hear it. I am thinking that if I leave, the things that Phillip said won't hold any water and she can live in peace."

Ralph couldn't think of a good argument against the words Timothy said, so he kept quiet.

"Besides, I will be able to make more money to send for her and the young'uns."

"Someday you might want to marry up with someone else."

"Never."

"Boy, you are young yet. Time changes everything," Ralph said as he spread out his bedroll and stretched out in it. "Throw some more wood on that fire. It is getting colder," he added.

Chapter 44

A piece of paper. That is all it is, and yet it rescues me from Phillip and his selfishness. She sat next to the fireplace and let the warmth penetrate her to the bone. The divorce papers lay in her lap while she watched the fire eat at the edges of the logs she had just placed in the fire. Emily watched various emotions play across Gracie's face. The children were down for their afternoon naps, so she had a chance to check on her own baby.

"The divorce is in effect?" she asked.

"Yes, and my deed of title is filed. No one can take it away now. I was just thinking that I need to make plans about planting and such. I can't always live off of Timothy's charity."

Emily nodded. Her voice was quiet, "I begin working for Dr. Johnson next week. I will be paid pretty well for being a nurse. You don't have to worry so much about money, dear."

"I know, I just need to get out of town to get away from the gossip. Phillip injured me more with his lies than he ever did with his fists. If I am out of sight, maybe the rumors will die down before the children get older."

Emily stood in front of the mantle and wound the mantle clock slowly. She placed the large brass key next to it. Her actions were deliberate while she thought of what to say, "Baby girl, I can't live at the farm with you.

Do you know that? I will be working. How will you manage?"

"I just know I have to leave so that I can breathe. Even when I sit on the porch, I see people gawking at me when they pass by. It is more difficult than I thought it would be. Now, with the divorce, there is bound to be more trouble. Even so, it will be spring before I can live at the farm."

A soft knock sounded at the door. Emily answered it and urged Mary Forrester, "Come inside. The weather is biting cold."

"Thank you. I just came to see how all of you are." Her eyes fell on the papers on Gracie's lap.

"These are the papers saying that I am divorced."

"Maybe now Phillip can't hurt you anymore."

Gracie shook her head, "He will always find a way." She stood and placed the papers on a small table in the parlor.

"I thought you might want to know that Timothy has headed out for Texas," Mary said.

"Texas, why Texas?" Emily asked.

Gracie straightened her shoulders and took a determined breath. She turned toward Mary and offered her a seat next to the rocker where she had been sitting.

"Thank you, Gracie. It seems that he has gotten together some fellers and they are going to round up some longhorn cattle down there. In fact, John has thrown in with him along with Ted Young. It will take them between twenty-five to a hundred days.

"Goodness sakes, that might be over three months," Emily said.

"Timothy said that they may have to go as far as the San Antonio area to get them, but they are free for the taking. They will drive them on to Dodge City, Kansas to the railhead there, where they will sell them and split the profit. He is aiming to make something of himself. He wants to have a spread of his own some day," Mary said.

"Gracie, he could raise cattle on your place!" Emily said enthusiastically.

"Ma, what are you talking about?"

"Mary, does Timothy own any land?" Emily asked.

Mary muttered, "Ah...no..."

"You have land. If he gets cattle, you could buy them to raise on your place. You could make the farm into a cattle ranch. I am sure that, since you controlled those mules on the mule team, taking care of a few head of cattle wouldn't be any harder than that."

Mary joined in the conversation, "That's right! Miranda and Ted ...and Timothy, for that matter, could teach you what all you need to know about running a cattle ranch."

Emily interrupted, "Have you thought about buying the land the judge forced you to give to Gus? He has no need for it and it is adjacent to your house and acreage. It just was not right that Phillip gambled it away."

"Wait! Wait, this is crazy!" Gracie swung around from Mary to Emily, saying, "Do you really think I could do it?"

Mary chimed in, "Of course you could do it. I will send word to Timothy and ask him to bring the second batch of longhorns to you. 'Course, I will ask him his opinion on the matter, but really, it is a business transaction and he has no say in it."

Gracie sat down hard on the rocker and mused, "Me, a rancher? If Miranda can do it, I can."

Chapter 45

Slim had been a drover for more than a dozen trips to Dodge City. The men wondered if he even had a last name. As Timothy, John, and Ted ate the regular campfire grub, he taught them the ways of the longhorn and what to expect on the cattle drive.

"We will have to scour the brush to find those ornery critters. They are tough varmints. The sicknesses that plague other breeds of cattle don't seem to bother them. We will only make ten to fifteen miles per day on the drive. They won't go into a tight formation. They tend to trail in a string. If we are able to round up two to three thousand head, they will be stretched out for a mile or two."

Timothy listened intently. He was glad that Ted and John wanted to try their hand at rounding up the wild Texas cattle. He was sorry that Ralph couldn't join them, but he was needed on Ted's ranch. They all wanted to go along for the money and to learn the ways of the cattle drive. After they sold the cattle in Dodge City, they wanted to make another trip to build herds in Colorado.

There were nine of them on the trail so far. They needed a cook and two more drovers. Ted would be the wrangler because he was a horse expert.

He would handle the remuda. It would be spare horses for all the crew. Each crew member needed eight to ten horses, so the number of horses he was responsible for would grow to over one hundred and possibly one hundred twenty. Ted, John, and Timothy would split the profit. The cook would earn sixty dollars a month and the drovers, known as thirty dollar men, would be paid per month on the trail. Slim was fine with the pay of a drover so they gave Slim the lofty position of trail boss. He balked at riding drag, so as trail boss, he wouldn't have to take that post. The position of riding drag rotated between all the drovers. It was a unique situation, but the other drovers wouldn't know the difference. To them, Timothy and John were just drovers.

"Now jist anything can spook those critters. It could be lightning, a loud noise, or even the smell of ole John's perfume," Slim laughed and slapped his leg when he made the joke.

"What do you mean?" John asked.

"I am jist saying that anything out of the ordinary way of things can set them off. When they take out in a stampede, they can go crazy and run over anything and everything," Slim continued, "...only thang thet can git them to come under control is to turn the herd to the mill."

"Turn the herd?" Ted asked.

"Drovers closest to the front of the herd will get in front of the leaders and force them to turn to the right.

First off, it will be a loose circle, but all the hands keep turning them into a tighter and tighter bunch. Eventually, they don't think they have anywhere to go, so they stop."

Timothy wondered how much damage two thousand wild longhorns could do until they were put under control. The few hundred that they had rounded up so far were hard enough to handle.

"I know a feller that makes a good cook. He has his own chuck wagon and mules to pull it. He hates drivin' oxen. He hates a lot of things. The only reason he might be available is...well...he is as mean as a buzzard. He ain't exactly the best at doctoring, but he knows the regular remedies. He lives here along the Canadian river. He is called Bones."

Ted laughed and said, "That don't say much for his cooking."

"One thang you gotta remember about Bones, he don't cotton to kiddin'. He has been known to leave in the middle of a job for no more than a complaint about his Pecos strawberries." Slim noticed Timothy's blank stare and explained, "they're beans...bullets are biscuits...chuck wagon chicken is bacon...and if you know what's good fer ya, you jist eat and keep your mouth shut if it don't measure up to your woman's cookin'. Got it?"

"Sure 'nuff," John said in an exaggerated drawl.

"Listen, feller, it would do you good to watch that smart alecky way you have of talkin'. It is plain as the nose on your face that you and your nephew there ain't from these parts.

Don't be makin' light of folks 'round here."

"I understand. No offense intended, Slim," John said.

"None taken. You jist need to get yourself a wagon for the calves that are born on the trail. They will be marked with a number put in it. So that the scent don't git all mixed up 'tween 'em, you will number the feed sacks and put each calf in the same feed sack to ride in the wagon during the day and let 'em out fer the night so that they can find their mama and feed. We can fit forty calves in one wagon."

Timothy couldn't help but ask, "Why does the scent matter?"

Slim gave him a withering look and spoke through gritted teeth, "Their mama won't let 'em feed if she ain't sure it her calf. She knows its scent."

They finished the last pot of coffee and bedded down under a full moon.

"Somebody turn out the light!" Slim said chuckling at the joke he made.

*****

By the end of the month, they had gathered the rest of the herd and found Bones, who was all too happy to sign on. Ted and John made a quick trip to a nearby town to finish getting supplies. The telegraph office was their first stop. Each sent a telegram to their wife saying they needed a quick response as they were there for only a few hours.

They loaded up on extra blankets, coal oil, salt, pepper, flour, and sugar.

John waited while Ted asked the clerk at the telegraph office if he had an answer yet. Miranda had responded.

Ted,
Glad you are starting to Dodge now. Praying for God's speed. We love and miss you.- Miranda

John took his turn to speak to the clerk. "Would there be anything for John Forrester?"

"Yes, here you go."

John,
Happy for you. Gracie wants to buy fifty head of cattle. Love you. - Mary

John reread the telegram. This was a new development. He would need to show this to Timothy. Ted saw the look on John's face. "Is something wrong?" he asked.

"Gracie is interested in buying cattle."

"How many?"

"...fifty head."

"We will need to have a talk with Timothy about this."

John drove the wagon loaded with the last of the supplies and tied his horse to the back while Ted rode along side.

They saw the dust from the herd that was bedded down for the night before they rode up.

"We might sell her the calves that are born on the drive. Slim said there are around forty or so head by the end of the trail," John said.

"That there is a really good idea," Ted agreed.

Chapter 46

Tex Sanders, Sheriff Moore's deputy, banged on Emily's front door. Spring was coming late in Colorado and he wished for one of the occupants of the house to hurry and open the door so that he could get on with his duties.

Emily opened the door. "Come in, Deputy Sanders," she said.

"Is Mrs. Masters here?"

"Gracie, the deputy is here to see you," Emily called.

Gracie wiped her hands on her apron as she emerged from the kitchen. "Mr. Sanders?"

"Sheriff Moore told me to give this to you. It is from the prison. Sheriff Moore already read it...ah...I did, too."

Her hands trembled as she unfolded the telegram.

Mrs. Masters,

This telegram is to inform you of the passing of your husband, Phillip Masters. He died as a result of an unfortunate incident at the prison.

Regards,
Warden Martin

"What happened to him?" she asked.

"Sheriff Moore contacted the warden and found out the details.

They are not something you should worry about."

"Please Deputy Sanders, I need to know what happened!"

The deputy stammered and restarted his explanation, "He made many enemies at the prison. No one will tell who his killer was. He was stabbed many times with a sharpened stick made from a chair rung. It happened during the evening meal. None of the prisoners allowed the doctor near him to tend his wounds until it was too late. I am sorry to say that he was a hated man."

"I see," Gracie could hardly believe that he had been murdered, "Will anyone be charged with his murder?"

"Even the warden is glad he is gone. I am sorry, ma'am, no one cares who killed him."

Wayne ran to his mama, "Who is that, mama?" he asked.

"This is Deputy Sanders," she explained.

"I need to go, Mrs. Masters...Mrs. Randalll."

"Goodbye, Mr. Sanders," Emily said.

Gracie held her little son close. The boy loved his papa so she needed to be careful with how she told him of his death. "Wayne, Papa went away, remember?"

He nodded.

"Papa has gone to heaven."

"Like he did before when he got his legs off?" he asked.

"No, sweetie, he won't be back to see you again. He is gone."

Wayne looked at his mama and put his arms around her neck. "Don't cry. Papa is gone. Pam Paw is in heaven now."

"Yes, your grandpa is in heaven and your papa is gone and he isn't coming back," she said it and the realization that Phillip would never be back to hurt anyone ever again became real to her. Tears threatened. She was sorry that he was such a miserable man that not even the law wanted to know who his killer was, but that was the kind of man he was.

*****

"Now she is free to swoop down on some unsuspecting man," a large woman with a bitter face said.

"She probably has her sights on her old lover," the lady who owned the dress shop where they stood said.

The first woman clicked her tongue. "Millie, that Timothy Forrester is a cad to romance another man's wife."

"Didn't you know that Gracie is a divorced woman? It isn't bad enough that she caused Mr. Masters to lose his legs, but she divorced the poor man while he was in prison!"

"He said that Timothy is the new baby's father..."

"Ladies! Ladies, I am horrified! Where is your Christian charity?" Pastor Reynolds heard the exchange and put them in their place. "He who is without sin, cast the first stone!"

The heavy set woman quickly stomped out of the shop leaving her accomplice to face the pastor alone.

"Millie Burnett, I never knew you to have a harsh tongue."

"I...ah..Pastor Reynolds, you have to admit that Mrs. Masters has been...well...less than Christian."

The good pastor squinted and pierced through her hard heart. He asked, "What unchristian thing was it? Was it taking care of her children's home and land, being abused by that brutish man, or her husband shooting to kill her and killing her father instead? Millie, your daughter, is about Gracie's age. Would you want her to have married Phillip Masters? She went to school with him as a child. What does she say about this 'innocent' man?"

"Forgive me, Pastor."

The frown remained on his brow. "Next time you join in on murdering someone with your tongue, remember that the Lord can hear you and does not approve. I may not hear you next time, but He is everywhere present. Do I make myself clear?" he asked as he left the shop without the parcel his wife asked him to pick up for her.

Chapter 47

John Forrester found himself at the chuck wagon again after supper. His smithing skills were in high demand on this particular trail. It seemed that the gear Bones owned was of the run-down sort. He checked the wagon and harnesses over and did what he could to repair without doing anything that would startle the herd and cause a stampede. Bones shadowed him by watching over his shoulder to make sure the Easterner wasn't messing up his wagon. Bones had never been east of the Mississippi, but he figured that the folks there probably did things differently than he would.

He got a kick out of hearing the funny way John and Timothy talked. They seemed to be all right. They carried their share of the work and didn't complain about his cooking. Slim must have told them the what for about how to deal with him on the trail and that was good enough for him.

John had found that riding trail was far less exciting than rumors of the "Wild West" had been depicted. He was relieved that they had not encountered fire or flood. The ornery beasts were wild enough for his taste. For the most part, he enjoyed the experience, except when it came to riding drag. The cattle could send dust up enough to be seen for a mile.

Ted and Timothy were riding herd and singing softly to bed down the restless herd. The skies clouded over and it looked like they could be in for a storm. Ted had seen cattle stampede, but Timothy hadn't. Ted hoped it would stay that way.

Slim and the others were stretched out around the campfire. Not a man was asleep. They reclined with their boots on and their saddled horses nearby. The rest of the horses were fed, watered, and tied off. Ted had taken care of them before he took his turn watching over the herd.

The longhorns were fidgety tonight and it wouldn't take much to get them agitated. So far, the worst thing that the men had suffered was windburn. Their skin looked somewhat like red leather. He began humming the song Timothy sang, "Get along little dogies. It's time to settle down..."

Suddenly the hair on the back of his neck stood up. A flash of lightening hit a scraggly cottonwood tree; then he heard a thunder clap. It boomed loudly. There was no time to think. Horns jabbed. Horses screamed in agony and the race was on.

Ted ran Tramp to the front of the herd and pushed the lead steer to the right. They ran so fast it was hard to realize that they turned at all. It was slight, but maybe enough to count. He pushed against him again and it worked better. The others followed suit. He glanced over his shoulder and saw Timothy thrown from his horse. He couldn't get to him so he shouted a prayer, "God take care of that kid!"

John saw Timothy fall. Several of the cattle stomped him before he was able to get to him. He jumped down, threw Timothy over his shoulder, and ran a few steps with the herd until he came to a fallen log. He covered Timothy with his body as the cattle ran swiftly past them. The other drovers chased after the herd, attempting to keep them turning to the right. They crashed through brush and ran down a steep creek bed. It was dry and the dust was thick. He coughed, choking on it. Some of the wily cattle plunged to the left and ran up the dried-out pathway. Slim and the others kept after the rest of the herd and turned them until they were under submission, and stopped several miles short of what would have been downstream. Both men and animals were beat. Sweat, blood, and dirt covered all of them.

Red blood covered Timothy's pale face. John shook at the sight of the bright color against everything else that was covered with dirt. Bones ran upon them and brought his medical bag. He carried camphor and held it under the young man's nose. Timothy coughed and opened his swollen eyes. Bones traced his ribs and said, "At least two of them are busted. Your arms and legs are in one piece. You broke your nose." He looked up at John and declared, "The kid got by pretty light as far as injuries."

John pushed him into a sitting position and removed his shirt. Bones tied a wide strip of cloth around and around his torso.

A loud groan escaped from Timothy's throat. His breaths came in short spurts. It hurt to breathe in as much as it hurt to breathe out. The sensation brought back memories of some of the harsher beatings he endured at the hand of his father. He knew he would live, but he knew that the pain would last for days.

He opened his mouth to speak. The words came out in short bursts, "It's all right...been through before..."

"Hesh up, Kid, save your strength," Bones urged.

Slim rode up and joined them. After assessing the situation, he leaned down and crossed his arms on his saddle horn, giving them their next orders, "We need to keep the herd tight tonight. The creek bed will help hold 'em in. Bones, move the camp here. Ted, see to the remuda and stake them off here. We will double the night watch. First light, I want John, David, Zeb, and Ted to look for strays and collect the calves from their mamas. We might have lost a few as far as the herd ran. Grab some sleep while you can. Tim, can you ride?"

"Yep, I will pull my share of the work."

"Just do what you can," Slim said as he turned toward the herd.

*****

Dodge City, Kansas was a sight for sore eyes. Slim looked at the haggard bunch of men driving the longhorns into the large corrals in the stockyard.

They looked like they had been rode hard and put up wet, but they were good men.

Timothy and John had surprised him. He was sure they were tender foot in nature, only covered with western gear. They would show their soft underbelly as soon as things got tough. Fact was, they out-worked most of the seasoned hands in the outfit. They learned the necessary skills quickly and held up their end of the work.

He was always glad to reach the end of the trail. As soon as he got his pay, he would go about the necessary job of spending it. He sat on the top rail next to the man in charge of tallying up the pay for the herd. The man gave him a sheet of paper with the tally on it saying, "Take this inside, Mr. Mays will pay you."

"Thank 'ya kindly," he said as he jumped off the fence rail and sauntered into the building next to the corrals.

Ted and John fell into step with him and climbed the steps to the building. The man made quick work of the transaction and soon the cowboys were headed into the bustling cow town. The first order of business was paying the men their wages. Each quietly took his pay and quickly made for town.

Ted shook Slim's hand and pounded him on the shoulder. "We couldn't have done it without you. Would you consider another next year?"

"I'm in, jist holler when you need me. I'll say my goodbyes now."

"Goodbye, Slim," John said as he shook his hand.

Timothy found Ted and John in the bathhouse, soaking in tin tubs with soapy water up to their chins. He had almost forgotten what they looked like without layers of dirt on their faces. "Now, don't you two look like a couple of gents?" he teased.

Ted answered, "At least we don't look like the dirt devil who just came in here."

Timothy paid the proprietor and soon was soaking off the trail dirt. He climbed the stairs to the room he rented at the hotel and spread out on the bed. He was asleep as soon as his head hit the pillow. He dreamed of cattle and rivers, stampedes and cracked ribs, then...nothing.

Chapter 48

The merry little kitchen couldn't bring Mary Forrester out of her lonely mood. In the months since her marriage, she had found companionship that she had never experienced before in her life. John had not been an answer to prayer because she had never prayed to be married again. She sat at the table drinking cup after cup of coffee. The bleak winter sky did little to lighten her spirits. The day before had offered a promise of spring, but the clouds moved in and darkened the world yet again.

She took the calendar from the wall and counted the days down again. *He said twenty five to one hundred days before they get the cattle to Dodge City. That was after they were rounded up from the countryside. How many days will it take them to get from Dodge City to Trinidad?*

She blinked her eyes quickly. *They could be back any day!*

She looked around the room with a critical eye. The house had never shined so much. She had little else to do but clean. She had even laid by a large stack of split wood for the fires. It had been a long time since she had handled an axe, but the skill came back soon enough. At first her arms were sore, but after the soreness left, she found that she had developed strength. Her back became stronger, also.

Who would have realized that strenuous exercise like that could help her overcome her frequent back pain and headaches?

She hurriedly rolled a pie crust and found a jar of apples that she had put by on their first week of marriage. It would be ready for John to celebrate his homecoming.

She made bread and cinnamon rolls and started a large pot of beans in the cast iron Dutch oven. After she finished her preparations, she walked to Emily and Gracie's house to pass the day just in case the men took longer to return.

Gracie opened the door for her and gave her a hearty hug. "Mary, it is so good to see you."

"I just needed someone to talk to today. John should be home any time now. I have puttered around the house until I have plum wore out the floor."

"Have you heard word about what they think of me buying some of the herd?"

"I haven't heard from them since the first telegram. The calendar is all wrinkled up from me studying it over every day," Mary said.

Emily gave her a knowing smile. "It is hard for a newly-married woman to be apart from her husband for so long. John probably has his hands full, else he would have sent word," she said.

Gracie asked, "Your calendar says that it could be any day?"

"Yep, day after tomorrow at the latest. That is, if there hasn't been a tragedy."

*****

Ted drove the horses through the streets of Trinidad. After the rest of the hands were paid and headed to their homes, there were just the three men and their horses left. At that, thirty horses remained in the remuda. They stirred up a lot of dust and interest from the townspeople.

John would keep his horses at the stable. Timothy and Ted would take theirs to the ranch. Timothy drove the buckboard loaded with twenty-four calves that were born on the trail. The three had decided that it would be easier to handle the calves on the trail to Colorado and make the trip progress faster because they were carried in the buckboard. They would sell them to Gracie when she was ready.

It had been a successful adventure. The longhorns brought a good price at the Dodge City stockyards. If Gracie hadn't asked to purchase some of them, they would have sold the calves with their mamas.

The skies were dark, but Ted determined that spring had reached the Rockies in full force. There was grass for grazing and the ranch should be none the worse for him being gone these past three months. He was in a hurry to get to the ranch and left the cattle transaction for Timothy to handle, even though Ralph would have everything under control.

Timothy turned the wagon down the road to the Randall's house while Ted and John drove the horses toward John's livery stable. John opened the doors to the stable and led his horses inside.

Mary heard the approach of the riders. She was glad that the house was next door to John's livery stable. She stood on the porch and watched as Ted and John cut ten horses from the herd. They were sturdy little mustangs. Her eyes caught John's and she nodded her approval. Before he disappeared in the building, he waved to his friend. Ted tipped his hat with his gloved hand and drove the rest of the horses down the road to the ranch.

Mary jumped from the porch and followed him into the stable. John held out his arms and Mary leapt into them, smothering his face with kisses. "Hey there, woman, it appears that you missed me," he said, laughing.

"I did!"

He held her close and gave her a firm kiss. "Let's take care of these fellers and finish our hellos inside," he said.

She released him and opened the door to one of the stalls. It would hold two of the mustangs. He measured out a scoop of oats for each of them and set to pumping water for the buckets in each stall. "You got ten of them?" she asked.

"Yep, I may trade some of them for good riding stock to hire out. I want to keep a few of them in case I go on the trail again."

"Good idea."

"Let me haul the water. Will you feed all of them oats and hay?" he asked, "That water is too heavy for you to manage."

"You might be surprised. You haven't seen the stack of wood I split while you were gone."

John laughed loudly at her pronouncement. "If you keep that up, I may get spoiled," he teased.

"I love to spoil you."

They finished caring for the horses and stepped into the yard. John whistled when he saw the stack of firewood and exclaimed, "Boy howdy, you sure did chop some wood!"

She couldn't help the feeling of pride. "I made a feast for you," she said.

"All of this and a feast, too?" He reached for her hand and held it to his heart. It seemed to him that she had blossomed in the months he was gone. Her face was relaxed and smooth while her cornflower-blue eyes sparkled.

She leaned against him for a moment, then pulled him up through the door. Her heart pounded in her ears. "I love you so much," she breathed.

John lifted her into his arms and carried her to their room. His rich baritone voice filled the room with song:

"When I return in the spring to sweet Mary,
and look in her sparkling blue eyes,
I promise that I will stay always,
because I'm not good at goodbyes."
Mary covered her mouth in shock.

"I had no idea you could sing like that!" she squealed, "Where did you learn that song?"

"On the trail, my love. I tried to imagine the blue of your eyes and the curve of your mouth. Making up the song helped me pass the time and keep the herd settled at nightfall."

"Is there more?"

"I will sing the rest of it to you after supper, but for now I just want to kiss my wife."

Chapter 49

Baby Jane had finished nursing while Gracie sat on the porch watching Wayne and Hope play in the yard. She was proud that Wayne showed great love and attention to his little sister. He held her pudgy hand as she practiced her walking skills. When she began to place a dirt clod into her mouth, he pushed it out of her hand and spoke in a firm voice, "Hope, no no. Dirt is not good to eat."

She cried briefly, then smiled, revealing two bottom front teeth. She had slobbered down the front of her little dress. *It appears that she is still teething.* Gracie's thoughts diverted to the bawling of calves. She saw a familiar figure driving a wagon.

Gracie stood and wrapped Jane close to her breast while she hiked up her skirts and jogged to the wagon. Looking over the side of the buckboard, she spied the calves.

"What do you think of your herd?" Timothy asked as he jumped to the ground from the wagon seat.

"My herd?"

He pushed his hat to the back of his head. "They will be big in no time. You will want to let your herd build up for a while before you sell off many.

"I see," she said as she wrung her hands nervously. Tears shined in her eyes, and she made a brave attempt at a smile.

Her anxious movements were not lost on him. He searched his mind to decide how to keep her from panicking. He draped his arm around her shoulders and walked her to the back of the wagon. "They are hardy stock...I will help you as much as I can," he said.

She nodded.

"Did you get any fences built?"

"No...ah...I haven't had the money. I mean, money has been scarce. I don't know how I can even pay for the calves," she croaked the words out and burst into tears.

He folded her into his arms and stroked her back. "I paid for the cattle," he said in a soothing tone.

She looked into his face, shaking her head vigorously, "No! No, I can't let you do that! Don't you know that people think this baby is yours? There is talk all over town because you have been kind to me. I can't let you buy anything for me," she said between sobs.

"I can buy my wife anything I want to...that is, if you agree to be my wife!"

"You don't want to do that! People will never stop talking!"

He held her close and whispered in her ear, "I love you. People don't matter. I will fight them all to keep you safe."

She turned to answer. He leaned close and gingerly kissed her mouth. She blushed.

"You don't want to ruin your life by wedding me."

"You are the best thing that has ever happened to me. I cannot imagine my life without you," he said.

Chapter 50

Mary and John Forrester joined Emily, Gracie, her children, and Timothy in the courthouse. The judge looked over his spectacles at the people standing before him. "So, which of you are to be married today?" he asked.

Timothy took Gracie's hand and stepped forward, saying, "We are, sir."

"I see that your papers are in order and you have witnesses, so let's begin. We are gathered here in the sight of God and these witnesses to join this man and this woman in holy matrimony. Marriage is an honorable state in which those who partake should take it on in all solemnity of mind.

Timothy Forrester, do you take this woman to be your lawfully wedded wife? Do you swear to love her, protect her, and honor her until the end of your life?"

"I do."

"Gracie Masters, do you take this man to be your lawfully wedded husband? Do you promise to love him, obey him, and honor him as long as you both shall live?"

"I do."

"I pronounce that you are husband and wife. Mr. Forrester, you may kiss your bride."

After Timothy and Gracie sealed their vows with a kiss, their loved ones swarmed around them with congratulations and best wishes.

Timothy picked up Wayne and put him on his shoulders to ride all the way to the Randall's house. Emily carried Jane, and Mary held Hope's hand.

John called out to the bride and groom, "It may take us a bit to arrive, but don't eat any wedding cake until we get there."

Timothy and Grace walked down the boardwalk on the way to the house. Pastor Reynolds stepped out of the pie shop and shook Timothy's hand. He gave Gracie a quick hug. Other shopkeepers and friends followed suit. Some of the more diligent gossips turned away abruptly, but overall, the attitude of the onlookers was festive.

Hope and Wayne waved at everyone who looked their way. Wayne yelled loudly, "We have a new papa! See my papa?"

Timothy's heart felt like it would burst with joy. This little boy riding on his shoulders would never know a moment of torture from his hands. He would show Wayne how to be a man. The plans he had for these children and their mother were greater than anything he had ever dared dream for himself. He felt as if he were dreaming. *Dear God, if I am dreaming, don't let me ever wake up!*

The wedding supper was the best he had ever eaten. The table was heaped up with fried chicken, mashed potatoes, greens, cooked carrots, fresh bread, and beans. Ted and Miranda, Fred and Nan, Dr. Johnson and several other friends joined them for the celebration.

After everyone had eaten their fill and the wedding cake was finished, Timothy and Gracie took the children with them to the farm. As they came into the yard, the wagon rolled to a stop. Timothy helped Gracie from the wagon seat. Jane slept and Gracie carried her inside to place her in the cradle. Wayne and Hope slept in the back of the wagon. Timothy carried each to his bed.

Wayne opened his eyes sleepily. Timothy placed his hands over his eyes and whispered, "Go ahead and sleep, partner. We have a lot to do tomorrow."

The boy sighed contentedly and turned on his side, continuing in deep slumber. Hope found her thumb and sucked loudly in the nearby bed. Timothy pulled the covers to her chin. *I'm their Pa!*

He shut the door noiselessly and found Gracie standing next to the table. He followed her gaze and looked around the room. "You did a good job cleaning up the place," he said.

She turned and gave him a nervous smile. "Adding the lean-to was a good idea. You worked very hard."

"It was a labor of love," he said quietly.

She studied his face. His brows knit together in thought, giving him a serious look. He caught the look of concern in her eyes and took her by the hand. He led her to a chair at the table. He pulled out the one next to her and sat in it.

He took the Bible that lay in the middle of the table and, clearing his throat, he timidly poured out his heart to her, "Gracie, in all my life the only person who cared whether I lived or died was Uncle John.

He saved my life. I will always be grateful to him for that. It had never entered my dreams to think that I would have a family of my own. Actually, I never thought I would survive childhood." Tears threatened, so he blinked quickly. Gracie reached across the table to his rough hands and stroked them gently. He continued, "When Phillip was killed in prison, I knew that I wanted to be a father to the young'uns and a husband to you, but I didn't know if I could learn how. My pa was cruel and never spoke a kind word to me until the end of his life, so I figured I was damaged merchandise and had nothing to offer to you.

"One night, on the cattle trail, Ted saw me being all melancholy and... he showed me some Scriptures about how God said He would be a Father to the fatherless. God would show me what to do. After talking this over with Ted, he asked me if I wanted to make plans for a life with you. It was then that I knew I didn't want to live another day without you in my plans.

"He left me then, and I got out this Bible. He had marked this verse with a bit of leather. It was in Jeremiah 29:11. Let me read it to you:

"'I know the thoughts that I think toward you, saith the Lord, thoughts of peace and not of evil, to give you an expected end. Then shall ye call upon me, and ye shall go and pray unto me, and I will hearken unto you. And ye shall seek me, and find me, when ye shall search for me with all your heart. And I will be found of you, saith the Lord.'

"It helped me to know that God has plans for me and those plans are for something good in my life. You are the best thing that I could even imagine...you and the children. I know that if I don't know what to do, God will help me."

Gracie rose out of the chair and nestled on Timothy's lap. She pushed his dark hair back off his smooth forehead and planted a kiss, breathing her words, "Timothy, welcome home."

The End

You may enjoy a sampling of the first book in the new Series:
Rescued...A Series of Hope
Book I - Some Happy Day

Some Happy Day

Constance Brooks settled her large brown eyes on
the desperate man sitting across the desk from her. The
child sleeping with her face nestled in his neck was
unaware of the transfer that was about to take place. Her
sister stood wide-eyed as she listened intently to the
conversation between Miss Brooks and her father. "I
can't do it anymore! Their mother is dead and I have to
work. These children will be better off with you than
being on their own while I work in the mines."

The young woman noted the tears welling up in the
six-year-old girl's eyes. "When did your wife pass?"

"Last week." The man rubbed the stubble on his
chin.

"Is this to be a permanent or temporary situation?"
Constance looked intently at him.

"You might as well adopt them out. I don't see my
life going better in the future."

Constance swallowed the lump in her tightening
throat. "What are their names and ages, sir?"

"Becky here is six and Ruth is two. They are mostly
quiet, but they tend to cry since their mama passed."

"Of course, Mr. Jamison please consider returning to
retrieve them someday soon. Life at the orphanage is hard
on little ones." Constance fought the emotions welling up
in her heart.

"Just get them a good home, Miss." The man stood,
slung the sleeping toddler down onto the chair and
stepped quickly out of the room.

Becky rushed to her sister and placed her arm around the tiny shoulders while the little one continued to slumber. Constance looked into the little troubled eyes. "Becky, I will take you to my room until daybreak. I don't want to disturb the other children and I want to help you get accustomed to your situation." Becky nodded dumbly.

No sooner had Constance placed the confused child and baby into her bed, than a brusque knock sounded at her door. "Constance, come to my office at once!"

If you have enjoyed this book, please write a review for it on amazon.com or goodreads.com or even on your profile page on facebook. I appreciate it so much when you share your books with friends and/or tell them about my writing. It really does help a lot.

You can contact me at elainelittau.com or nansjourney.blogspot.com.

I can be found on twitter as nansjourney.

I would love to hear from you.

Elaine Littau

ABOUT THE AUTHOR

Elaine Littau is the best selling author of five published books and many magazine and newspaper articles. She is a mentor/coach for other authors and enjoys teaching book marketing techniques as well as public speaking for groups. Many enjoy listening to her humorous take on life. Even the most simple activity takes on a life of it's own when Elaine is involved in the telling of it. Some of her favorite events have been speaking to young people about pursuing their dreams. She has been a church secretary, led women's groups, taught pre-school and Sunday school, and was a mentor for the M.O.P. S. (Mothers of Preschoolers) group in her community.

Her writings have also received recognition: "Nan's Journey"- Named Best Christian Historical Fiction 2008 by Christian Story Tellers and "Luke's Legacy"- Honorable Mention Christian Historical Fiction 2010 by Christian Story Tellers.

Elaine and Terry, her husband since March 1, 1975, reside on a small acreage near Perryton, Texas where they enjoy spending time with family and friends. They raised three sons and now enjoy three daughters-in-law and four grandchildren with another due at the beginning of 2012.

Made in the USA
Charleston, SC
24 November 2011